ERLE STANLEY GARDNER

- Cited by the *Guinness Book of World Records* as the #1 best-selling writer of all time!

- Author of more than 150 clever, authentic, and sophisticated mystery novels!

- Creater of the amazing Perry Mason, the savvy Della Street, and dynamite detective Paul Drake!

- THE ONLY AUTHOR WHO OUT-SELLS AGATHA CHRISTIE, HAROLD ROBBINS, BARBARA CARTLAND, AND LOUIS L'AMOUR *COMBINED!*

Why?

Because he writes the best, most fascinating whodunits of all!

You'll want to read every one of them, from
BALLANTINE BOOKS

Also by Erle Stanley Gardner
Published by Ballantine Books:

The Case of the

Borrowed Brunette

Erle Stanley Gardner

BALLANTINE BOOKS • NEW YORK

Cast of Characters

PERRY MASON—trial lawyer, indefatigable student of human nature 1

DELLA STREET—Mason's confidential secretary ... 1

CORA FELTON—an unborrowed brunette 3

"Mr. Hines's representative" 6

GERTIE—Mason's receptionist and telephone operator 11

ADELLE WINTERS—chaperone of the borrowed brunette 12

ROBERT DOVER HINES—temporary occupant of a Siglet Manor apartment 26

EVA MARTELL—the borrowed brunette 29

HELEN REEDLEY—high-voltage spouse of Orville Reedley 41

PAUL DRAKE—head of private detective agency .. 52

ORVILLE L. REEDLEY—high-powered, restless, estranged husband of Helen Reedley 62

v

HARRY GULLING—the D.A.'s wheel-horse and front man 95

MAE BAGLEY—rooming-house manager 105

FRANK HOLT—one of Paul Drake's operatives ... 110

CARLOTTA TIPTON—Siglet Manor glamour girl ... 111

ARTHUR CLOVIS—assistant cashier at Orville Reedley's bank 149

JUDGE HOMER C. LINDALE—presiding judge 159

SAMUEL DIXON—radio-car officer 160

THOMAS FOLSOM—private detective 171

ALFRED KORBEL—police expert on ballistics and fingerprinting 179

1

At this hour, Adams Street was a pedestrian's no man's land. Stretching between the business and the residential districts, it was far enough from the shopping centers so that people having occasion to use the street walked only far enough to make connections with the nearest streetcar or bus.

Perry Mason, having concluded a difficult case in one of the outlying courts, was driving slowly, relaxing after the nerve strain of a courtroom battle. Della Street, instinctively knowing Mason's moods, as befitted a good secretary, remained silent.

Mason was always interested in people, and his eyes occasionally strayed from the road ahead when breaks in traffic enabled him to scrutinize such pedestrians as were on the street. Now he slowed, moved over to the extreme right-hand lane of traffic. The car was rolling along at a scant fifteen miles an hour.

"Notice it, Della?" he asked.

"What?"

"The street corners."

"What about them?"

"The brunettes."

She laughed. "Window-shopping?"

"No, no," Mason said impatiently. "Look at them. Every street corner has a brunette standing waiting. They're all dressed in dark clothes, all wear some sort of a fur around the neck.—Here's another one at this corner. Notice her now as we pass."

Della Street studied the trim brunette who was standing

as though waiting for a streetcar on a street where there were no streetcar tracks.

"Neat," she said.

Mason said, "Bet you five bucks there's another one at the next corner."

"No takers."

The next corner also held a brunette almost identical in appearance. She too was wearing a dark dress with silver foxes around her neck.

"How long," Della Street asked, "has this been going on?"

Mason said, "I'm ashamed to say I don't know. I've seen five or six of them. Let's go back and see how many of them there are."

Mason watched his opportunity, made a U-turn, and sped back along the boulevard. Della Street, knowing how much of his success was due to his ability to make instantaneous appraisals of character, and to a sympathetic understanding of human nature, saw nothing unusual in the fact that Mason should interrupt a busy schedule to count the brunettes who were standing at corners on the south side of Adams Street.

"Well," Mason said at length, "we seem to have passed them. I count eight."

"Check," she said smiling.

"And Lord knows how many more were ahead of us there when we turned back. What say, Della? Do we take a chance on having this first one cry, 'Wolf, wolf'?"

"You can't be ruled off for trying," Della said.

Mason once more made a U-turn.

"There's a parking space there right next to the corner," Della Street said. "We can't overlook an opportunity like that."

"Can't for a fact," Mason admitted, swinging his car in close to the curb.

The brunette flashed them a glance of quick interest, then

became studiously absorbed in watching the traffic, ignoring their obvious scrutiny.

As Mason got out of the automobile he said, "You'd better come along to lend an air of quasi-respectability to this, Della."

Della Street slid out of the car with a quick, lithe motion and inserted her hand in Mason's arm.

Mason walked up to the young woman and raised his hat.

The girl instantly swung toward him and flashed a smile. "Are you Mr. Hines?" she asked.

"The great temptation is to say yes," Mason told her.

She ceased smiling. Her eyes, becoming wary, sized up Mason and Della Street. "Surely not one of those things," she said coldly.

"Hardly," Della Street said, assuming her most friendly manner.

The girl said abruptly to Perry Mason, "Is this a joke? I've seen you before. I know you . . . Oh," she said, "now I have it. I saw you in court. You're Perry Mason, the lawyer."

Della Street nodded. "And I'm his secretary. Mr. Mason couldn't help wondering about all of you being here."

"All of us?"

"Every street corner for blocks," Mason said, "has a brunette wearing a dark dress and a fur."

"How many blocks?"

"At least eight."

"Yes, I'd supposed there'd be quite a few applicants."

"Know any of them?" Mason asked.

She shook her head, then after a moment said, "I know one of them—my roommate and pal, Eva Martell. I'm Cora Felton."

"And I'm Della Street," Della said, and then added laughingly, "And now that we're acquainted, would you mind telling us what it's all about? Mr. Mason won't settle down to work as long as he has an unexplained mystery on his mind."

Cora Felton said, "It's a mystery to me too. Did you by any chance see the ad?"

Mason shook his head.

She opened her purse, took out a want ad that had been torn from a paper, and handed it to Mason. "It started with this," she said. The ad read:

WANTED: Neat, attractive brunette, age twenty-three to twenty-five, height five feet four and one-half inches, weight one hundred and eleven pounds, waist measurement twenty-four inches, bust measurement thirty-two. Weight and measurements must be absolutely exact, and the applicant must be free for colorful, adventurous work that will pay fifty dollars a day for a minimum of five days, maximum of six months. Successful applicant may select her own chaperone, who will be with her constantly during period of employment at salary of twenty dollars a day and expenses. Telephone Drexberry 5236 and ask for Mr. Hines.

"And you applied for the job?" Mason asked.

"Yes."

"By telephone?"

"That's right."

"And talked with Mr. Hines?"

"I talked with a man who said he was Mr. Hines's representative. He said that I was to wear a dark suit and be sure to have some sort of fluffy fur around my neck, go to this corner promptly at four o'clock this afternoon, and wait here until five. In the event I was not selected, I would be given ten dollars for my trouble."

"When did you answer the ad?"

"About eleven o'clock this morning."

"It was in this morning's paper?"

"Yes. That is, it was in a trade paper widely read by actresses. It was published this morning."

"I presume you were advised that there were other applicants?"

She laughed and said, "I knew it. Within an hour after I

telephoned, my roommate—Eva Martell—came in and I told her about it, and *she* rang up. She's a brunette of almost exactly my build. We can wear each other's clothes, even to gloves and shoes."

"And what did Mr. Hines tell her?"

"Not Mr. Hines—the man who said he was Mr. Hines's representative. He told Eva to meet him at four o'clock at a point four blocks farther down the street. So there must have been three other applicants accepted for consideration between the time I applied and the time she phoned."

Mason looked at his watch. "Well, it's five minutes to five now. You've been here since four?"

"That's right."

"Notice anything unusual? Anyone looking you over?"

She laughed at him and said, "Heavens, Mr. Mason, everyone in the city has been looking me over. I never felt so conspicuous in my life. I've had wolves bark at me, coyotes yelp, and airedales whistle. People on foot have tried picking me up. People in automobiles have offered to take me wherever I wanted to go, and other people have just twisted their necks half off."

"And yet you haven't been asked to take the job?"

"Not even a tumble from Mr. Hines. I suppose, of course, he must either have looked me over, or had his representative do so. When I decided to come here, I made up my mind I'd get a good look at whoever was sizing me up. But—well, you just take any girl who answers that description and let her stand unescorted on a street corner such as this for an hour, and you'll see how much chance she'd have to separate the wheat from the chaff!"

Mason nodded. "Very, very shrewd," he said, admiringly.

"What was?"

"The way Hines prevented you girls from spotting him when he was sizing you up. He was very careful to select a street that was just right for his purpose—not so far out as to frighten you, not so close to the shopping district that you would be inconspicuous in the crowd. As it was, this street was so public that you were willing to come here, yet sufficiently uncrowded so that every wolf would spot you. Hines could have walked past here two or three times, even stopped to make a pass at you, but you wouldn't be able to tell him from the rest of the wolves."

"Yes, I suppose so."

"It was very cleverly handled. But that ten-dollar pay-off is interesting, and it's about due. I wonder if you'd have any objection if we waited to see . . ."

He broke off as a man, walking rapidly down the sidewalk, veered in toward the little group at the corner, raised his hat, and said, "Miss Felton?"

"Yes."

"I represent Mr. Hines, and I'm sorry to advise you that the vacancy had been filled. You are to receive ten dollars for your trouble in coming here, and Mr. Hines asked me to see that you get this ten-dollar bill. Thank you. Good-by."

The man thrust the bill into Cora Felton's hand, raised his hat and started on down the street, his right hand dropping to his coat pocket, his left hand holding a card on which a list of names had been written.

"Hey, wait a minute," Cora Felton called. "I'd like to find out . . ."

He turned. "I'm sorry—that's all I know, Miss Felton. I was given that message to deliver. I don't even know what it means myself. Good afternoon." And he proceeded rapidly across the street.

"Can you beat that?" Cora Felton said. And then added philosophically, "Well, I'm ten bucks to the good anyway. He could have gypped me out of that easy as not."

Mason said, "I'm going on down the street. How would you like to jump in the car, drive four blocks down to where your friend is waiting, and get a chance to interview Mr. Hines's representative once more?"

Her eyes smiled into his. "Say, that's something! I'd love it."

"Hop in," Mason invited.

They drove on down Adams Street in time to see the man paying off the girl at the next corner.

"It'll be two more streets," Cora Felton said.

Mason drove his car down past two more corners where brunettes were waiting and pulled in close to the curb as he approached the third corner.

Cora Felton said, "She'd be thrilled to death to meet you, Mr. Mason. She'll be right here . . . Why, that's funny—I don't see her."

Mason brought the car to a full stop. Cora Felton opened the door, looked carefully around on all four of the corners, and said with a laugh, "Well, she's gone home. She wasn't too enthusiastic about it anyway. Eva isn't the kind to stand around waiting on street corners.—Well, thanks a lot Mr. Mason, and I certainly enjoyed meeting you. I'll really have something to tell Eva when I get home."

Mason said, "I'm going toward town. Are you by any chance headed that way?"

"We have an apartment out on West Sixth Street. If you're going in that direction . . . I don't want to put you out any."

"That'll be fine. It's just as easy to go that way as any other."

Cora Felton settled back in the seat. "This is a real thrill. I'm gong to make Eva's eyes pop out. I'll probably beat her home."

Mason made time through traffic and brought his car to a stop in front of the apartment house.

"I don't suppose I could interest you folks in a drink?" Cora Felton asked, and then added, laughing, "You'd have an opportunity to meet the woman who was to have been our chaperone in case we landed the job. And you'd *really* get a kick out of her."

"Salty?" Mason asked.

"Salty *and* peppery! You know, in answering an ad like that you can't be sure what's in the wind. I was hoping I'd land it if only to be able to spring Adelle Winters on that Mr. Hines!"

Mason glanced at Della Street, then tentatively shut off the ignition on his car. "Tell me about Adelle Winters."

"Well, she's been a practical nurse. She's redheaded and chunky, and she wants to live her own life. She can't be bothered too much by rules and regulations, and for that very reason is probably one of the greatest liars in the world. Whenever people start questioning her about things she thinks are none of their business, or try to make her conform to some convention or law that she doesn't approve of, she proceeds to lie her way out with a great deal of ability and a perfectly clear conscience. She's a darned good liar."

"How old?" Mason asked.

"Oh, somewhere between fifty and sixty-five. You'd never know, and she won't tell.—Do come on up!"

"We will at that," Mason said. "Long enough for a cocktail and to meet Mrs. Winters.—You don't think Mr. Hines would have slipped anything over on *her*, he?"

"Mr. Hines definitely would *not* have slipped anything over on Aunt Adelle.—The apartment's on the third floor, and the elevator is automatic."

"You girls both looking for work?" Mason asked on the way up.

"That kind of work, yes. We're actresses—at least we think we are, or we thought we were before we came here. We've had a few jobs as extras in Hollywood and we've done some work as models. We're getting by okay, but we're interested in new contacts. That's how we happened to decide to answer that ad. It probably means a job as understudy somewhere. The way those measurements were listed in such detail, it must have been something like that."

Cora Felton fitted a latchkey to the apartment door, then turned with a little laugh and said, "Better let me look in first to make certain everybody's decent."

8

She held the door open and called out, "Company coming. Everybody dressed!"

There was no answer.

"Well, that's strange," she said. "Come on in. I guess there's no one home. Oh-oh, what's this?"

A note pinned to the table had caught her attention. She opened and read it, then passed it to Mason without a word.

Cora dear, I landed. I hadn't been there over ten minutes when Mr. Hines drove up, talked with me, said that I'd do, and asked me if I wanted a chaperone. *Did* I? I had him drive me up to the apartment here and pick up Aunt Adelle, also a few personal things.

It sounds terribly wacky and mysterious. I'm not certain that I like it, but I'm banking on Aunt Adelle to see us through. I wanted him to drive me up to your corner and pick you up and tell you what had happened. But he said nothing doing. It seems one of the rules of the job is that I'm not to communicate with any of my friends until after the job is finished, which apparently will be at the end of thirty days. I'm banking on Aunt Adelle, and she's banking on a .32-caliber revolver that has been her constant companion for years. In honor of the occasion she bought a fresh box of shells so as to be certain there won't be any misfire.

Don't worry about us. We'll be bringing home the bacon. You know Aunt Adelle!

Lovingly,
Eva

Mason handed back the note.

"What do you make of it?" Cora asked.

"The note?"

"No, the job."

9

"Are you sure Adelle Winters is thoroughly capable of taking care of herself?"

"Taking care of herself and Eva too," Cora said. "Anyhow, don't worry about Eva. She isn't going to be caught very far off first base.—What will you have? Manhattan or Martini?"

"A Manhattan," Mason said.

"Same here," Della Street said.

Cora Felton opened the icebox, took out a bottle of prepared cocktails, and poured three drinks.

"Well," Mason said, picking up his glass, "here's to crime!"

"*You* would!" Cora said.

2

On Thursday morning Gertie appeared in the doorway of Mason's private office just as Mason and Della Street were going through the mail. "Gosh, I'm sorry to butt in, Mr. Mason," she said, "but this was something I couldn't handle over the phone."

"What is it?"

Gertie's habitually wide grin seemed even broader than usual. "I told this party you didn't see people except by appointment, and she asked me how people got appointments. And while I was thinking that one over, she said, 'You go tell Mr. Mason that it's ten o'clock now and I want an appointment for five minutes after!' I thought Della might care to look her over."

Mason laughed. "Is she as determined as she sounds?"

"More so. She looks capable of just about anything."

"What does she want to see me about? Did she say?"

"Sure. She talks right up. She's a companion or an adopted aunt or something to a couple of girls, and she heard them talking about you—or one of them was talking about you. She said that you knew all about the case, but you just didn't know her."

"Did you get her name?" Mason asked.

"Uh-huh, it's Adelle Winters."

Mason shook his head. "It means nothing to me."

"Wait a minute!" Della Street exclaimed. "Adelle Winters! That's the woman who's the chaperone. Remember, Chief, the case of the brunettes on the street corners?"

"I remember now," Mason replied. "A man advertising

for brunettes, with one on every street corner. By all means, let's see what she looks like."

Gertie retired, and a moment later Adelle Winters—short squat, competent, and alert—came marching into the office.

"Good morning, Mrs. Winters," Mason said.

She regarded him with lively, suspicious eyes. "Humph! You're a lawyer. You're supposed to have a business office so you can see people. Ain't that right?"

"That's right," Mason said, smiling.

"Well, you'd better do something about that girl out there in the other office. Telling me you didn't see people without an appointment! So I asked her how people got the appointments in the first place if you don't see them—and that floored her. Now I want you to listen to what I have to say and I don't want you to send me a bill afterwards because I haven't any money to pay lawyers. So let's have that understood right at the start.—Who's that woman?"

"My secretary, Miss Street."

"Can you trust her?"

"I certainly hope so."

"So do I. Now, you've got to keep it secret about my being here."

"What's the necessity for secrecy?"

"Well, you'll understand when I tell you about it."

"Do sit down," Mason said. "It isn't often we have clients who are so disarmingly frank about the matter of our charges—though many of them doubtless have the same idea you do."

"Well, the way I look at things, there ain't no harm in coming right out and saying what you've got in mind. Having an understanding in the first place saves a lot of trouble. Now you gave Cora Felton a ride the day that Eva Martell was hired?"

Mason nodded.

"Cora told me about that, and I've seen your name in the papers a lot. Seems to me you're a mighty upstanding young man."

12

"Thank you."

"I wouldn't have come to you unless I thought you were. I wanted the best."

Mason bowed silent acknowledgment.

"Now this job we've got is the craziest job a body ever had, and Lord knows I've seen some funny stuff in my time. I've been a practical nurse for—well, for a good many years. I've nursed all sorts of people, including neurotics and crazy guys."

"And this is a nursing job?"

"Listen," she said. "Get this straight, because I don't want any misunderstanding about it. This job is a *murder* case."

"Someone is about to be murdered?" Mason asked.

"Someone *has* been murdered."

"Who?"

"A woman by the name of Helen Reedley."

"Who killed her?"

"Land sakes, *I* don't know! What do you suppose I'm coming to you for?"

"That's what I'm trying to get straightened out."

"Well, I'm coming to you because you're a lawyer and a smart one. And Eva Martell and Cora Felton are just like daughters of mine. They're no relation really, but I nursed their mothers when they were little tots and I've sort of kept my eye on them ever since."

"Now I understand it," Mason prompted, "Eva Martell was the one who was hired for this job."

"That's right."

"Suppose you tell me exactly what happened."

"Well, both of the girls went out to see if they could land the job. I told them that it sounded pretty screwy to me, but I also told them that if they could take their own chaperone they didn't have anything to worry about because I'd be on the job. And if some fellow thought he was going to pick himself up a nice cute chicken with an ad like that and pay a chaperone twenty dollars a day to keep her eyes closed, he had another guess coming.

"Well," she said, "I sat up there in the apartment waiting for the girls to come back. To tell you the truth, I didn't think that either of them would get the job—I didn't even think there *was* a job. But I sat around and waited. And then Eva came in all excited. There was a man with her. He said he wasn't Mr. Hines, but Mr. Hines's representative, and that Eva had been hired and that we had to get on the job at once. As I said, Eva was all excited. And I didn't blame her, because it would amount to a lot of money by the time *she* got paid and I got paid and all our expenses got paid! So it looked pretty good, and we started off."

"I arrived at the apartment very shortly after you'd left," Mason said. "I take it you got packed up in a hurry?"

"There wasn't any packing to do—that was the first screwy thing about it—just what personal stuff we could carry in an inconspicuous little handbag, he said. And what sort of bag do you suppose he meant, Mr. Mason?"

Mason raised his eybrows interrogatively.

"An ordinary, everyday shopping bag," she went on. "The man had brought it with him. He said that where we were going he didn't want us to be seen carrying any baggage. So we were to carry that shopping bag as though we'd been out getting some groceries."

"And then where did you go?" Mason asked.

"We went to a mighty nice little apartment. Not a swanky place but a real nice little up-to-date double apartment. Moved in just as though we owned the joint. Then the man said to me, 'Now, Mr. Hines has a lease on this apartment, but the lease is in the name of Helen Reedley and there's a clause in it saying that it can't be sublet; so, in order to keep from being put out, this young lady will go by the name of "Miss Helen Reedley." Tell everyone that's her name, and she must remember to answer anyone who calls her Miss Reedley.' He went on to explain to us about how tough it was to get apartments, and how the landlady was inclined to

14

be coöperative, but after all, she couldn't stand too much without losing her job. However, as long as Eva had the name of Helen Reedley, it would be all right."

"And what did you say to that?"

"It didn't fool me for a minute," she said truculently. "I knew there was some skulduggery afoot the minute he said that, but I wasn't going to say anything unless he got fresh. I was there as a chaperone, and I made up my mind I was going to do a good job of it. There wouldn't be any funny business going on with this Mr. Hines."

"Can you describe him?" Mason asked.

"He's somewhere around thirty, with dark hair and sort of pop eyes and glasses. Tall, and sort of milk-custardy."

"Evidently the one who showed up later and paid the women off."

"That's right. That's what Cora said when I described him to her."

"And so Eva Martell was installed in this apartment as Helen Reedley. Was there anything in the apartment?"

"Was there anything in the apartment!" Adelle Winters echoed. "I'll say there was something in the apartment! There was *everything* in there. Clothes, underwear, nylon stockings, lotions, creams—absolutely everything that a body could want. And this representative of Mr. Hines . . ."

"Did he ever give you his name?" Mason asked.

"What do you take me for?" she snorted. "That man was Mr. Hines himself! He was the one who put the ad in the paper and was behind the whole business. I'm sure of it."

"But he didn't ever give you his name?"

"No, he just kept saying 'Mr. Hines's representative.' And he certainly was a fast worker. He took us up to that apartment and told us to stay there until he got back—just make ourselves at home. Then he went dashing out, I suppose to tell the other girls the job had been filled. And then he came back maybe an hour and a half later to tell us the details."

"And what were the details?" Mason asked.

"Well in the first place, he told us we must break off completely from our past lives; we were to live in that apartment without having any connection with the outside world except such as he approved of. We were not to call any of our friends on the telephone, not to write any letters, not to try to communicate with them in any way."

"Did he say why?"

"No. That was part of the job, he said—that we would have to do it that way because it was part of the job. Eva Martell was to be Helen Reedley. I was to go by my own name and be there as a companion and nurse. Because the idea was to create the impression this Miss Reedley was sick and might get worse. She was to keep inside most of the time, and if people came to see her I was to tell 'em she was nervous and had given instructions that she couldn't see anyone; or, if they seemed to be old friends, I'd say she was out. If anyone called up on the telephone and asked to speak with Miss Reedley, I was to answer the phone, get the name and the number, and say that Miss Reedley would call back later. Then I was to call Mr. Hines and tell him about it. And that was all.

"What's more, Hines said that whenever we went out, Eva was to wear the clothes that were in the apartment—she wasn't to wear anything of her own. You can see now why the man wanted a girl of a certain height and certain other measurements—the whole job was to be one of impersonation."

Mason's eyes showed that he was interested. "How about you? How about *your* clothes?"

"Humph!" Adelle Winters snorted. "He said *I* didn't matter. He said I could wear what I had on no matter where I went. And I certainly gave him a piece of my mind about that. I told him he could see that I had some clothes or we'd walk off the job, both of us."

"So then?"

"Well, he finally gave me permission to go and get some

of my clothes. But he insisted on going with me. He said he would take the clothes and see that they were delivered to the apartment. And do you know how he intends to deliver them?"

"How?"

"He's going to pay a dry-cleaning establishment to bring them in on hangers as though they were some clothes we'd sent out! He's terribly particular about not having baggage of any sort moved into the apartment or out of it."

"About the real Helen Reedley's intimate friends? How are they to be handled?"

"Apparently the same way other calls are handled. If they ring up I'm supposed to get their names and tell them Miss Reedley is out, or sleeping, or something. Then I'm to call him."

"You've done that?"

"Twice, yes."

"And does he tell you to have Eva call them later?"

"No."

"And do the friends ring up again and ask why they weren't called?"

"So far they haven't. In case that ever happens, Mr. Hines says, I'm to tell them I gave Miss Reedley the message, but that she was rushing out to see her doctor and that she probably intends to call them from the doctors office."

"Then Hines has given you a telephone number?"

"That's right. The same one that was in that ad."

"Have you checked up to see if he's listed in the phone book?"

"Yes, but it's evidently an unlisted number."

"But if he's holding you there incommunicado," Mason said, "how does it happen that you have talked with Cora Felton and now have come here?"

"Humph! D'you think I'd let him pull anything like that on me? He and I went out for my clothes, and after I'd got them he took them and called a taxi. When I was inside it, he took the driver off a little way and gave him quite a talking to, and then handed him a bill. Then he raised his hat and said he'd see me at the apartment, that the cab driver knew where to go.

"Well, as soon as the driver started off, I asked him where he was going. He gave me the address all right. So then I told him I wanted to stop at a telephone and he smiled and said no, that he'd have to keep right on going. Well, one thing led to another, and finally I found out that Hines had told him I was a little simple-minded and forgetful and that if I ever got out on the street I wouldn't be able to find my way back home alone; that two or three times lately I've had to be located through the police. While I was perfectly harmless and didn't have any hallucinations or anything, I'd just lost part of my mind, and under no circumstances was he to trust me out of the car until he got to that address. Then he was to see that I went right upstairs into the apartment."

"So what did you do?" Mason asked.

"I proceeded to tell that cabby where he got off at! I explained the man was my son-in-law who was always playing practical jokes on me and that I'd pin his ears back when I got home. And I went on to show the driver that I knew my way perfectly well around the city by telling him every street and every turn we'd made since I got into the cab. Well, that convinced him all right, so pretty soon he agreed to stop and let me out—and I could telephone Cora. Sure enough, she was home. I told her the whole story over the telephone and she said that, just in case what I was thinking was true, I'd better go straight to you. She felt sure you'd know what to do because you were acquainted with the case already."

"And what *were* you thinking?" asked Mason.

Her glance was almost pitying. "Good heavens, Mr. Mason, you're a lawyer. Don't you know what it is—*yet?*"

Mason shook his head.

She snorted again. "Why, that man is no more Hines than

I am! He's Helen Reedley's husband. He's killed her and disposed of the body, and now he's working up some sort of scheme to prevent this from being known. So he's got Eva and me living there and pretending that everything's hunky-dory. Then after a while he'll tell us to say we're going away, and we'll pack up and get out, telling everybody we're going to Mexico City or some place."

"Who's everybody?"

"Why, all of the Reedley girl's friends."

"But don't you think that if any of her friends saw Eva Martell they'd know she wasn't Helen Reedley?"

"Of course they would, but evidently the kind of friends she has wouldn't come to her apartment without ringing up first. That's where all this sick business comes in. He can give out that his wife got worse in Mexico City and died there!"

Mason's nod was not one of agreement, but much the gesture of a man who doesn't want to waste time in profitless argument and so yields the point, leaving his mind free to concentrate.

Adelle Winters was going on. "I'm not so dumb—I wasn't born yesterday. That man has a key to the apartment, and he had the run of the whole place. He knows where everything in it is, right down to the smallest pair of silk panties. He knows his way around the apartment like nobody's business. I tell you he's *lived* there! He's got rid of this Reedley woman and needs time to dispose of the body and build up his scheme. That's why he's got us there—so that he can get out from under."

"Of course," Mason pointed out, frowning, "there are *some* points that don't check with that theory. In the first place, why would he leave so much evidence around? He could be traced through that ad looking for a brunette actress. In the second place, the story that you and Eva Martell would be able to tell would absolutely convict him. If he's gone that far, then he must intend to see that something happens to you—to *both* of you—just as soon as you've given him the alibi or whatever it is he wants. It would seem to me that he'd be more apt to be *planning* to kill her, and then to give himself an alibi by showing she was in her apartment at the very time police claim he was doing the killing. . . . But how would he show *that?*"

"You listen to me, young man! You can bet your bottom dollar there's a murder wrapped up in this. Why, even her purse is there!"

Mason raised skeptical eyebrows. "Probably an old purse she's stopped using and—"

"No such thing. It's her purse, her very own purse!"

"How do you know?"

"Why, it's got her things in it."

"What things?"

"Lipstick, compact, handkerchief, visiting cards, a coin purse with three dollars in silver and thirty-two dollars in currency, a pair of dark kid gloves, and a leather key-container with half a dozen keys in it."

"Keys to the apartment?" Mason asked.

"One of them is."

"What are the others to?"

"I don't know."

"What do they look like?"

"I don't think they're safety-deposit keys, if that's what you mean. They look just like ordinary door keys. Not the old-fashioned kind, but the kind with the indentations that slips right into the lock and then turns."

"Social Security number?" Mason asked.

"No. No Social Security card."

"Driver's license?"

"No. No driver's license."

"That purse sounds like a plant to me, Mrs. Winters."

"Well, it *could* be, but I don't think it is. I tell you, that Reedley woman has been murdered. I know it just as well as I know I'm sitting here. You surely must have heard of feminine intuition?"

"I have," Mason replied with a grin, "but the police haven't!"

"Well, I've had that feeling ever since I walked into the apartment. It's a murder apartment, and Eva Martell and I are acting as cover-ups for a murder. Now, you're a lawyer and you're responsible. If you tell me that what we're doing isn't illegal and that we're to go right ahead with it, why, then young man, *you* can assume the responsibility—"

"Wait a minute, wait a minute," Mason laughed. "In the first place, you're approaching me simply because I talked with Cora Felton on the street. You haven't any money to pay lawyers and don't intend to pay me. I'm not a public official. If you want to be sure that you're in the clear, my advice to you is to go to the police."

She snorted again. "I'd cut a pretty figure going to the police and trying to tell them about my suspicions. I don't know what a lawyer's for if it isn't to advise people."

Della Street's telephone rang. She glanced questioningly at Mason, and, at his nod, picked up the receiver. "Yes, this is Mr. Mason's confidential secretary talking. . . . Who? . . . Oh, yes . . . How are you this morning? . . . Why, yes. . . . Well, nothing definite yet. . . . Just hold the line, please."

Della placed the receiver on the desk, drew a memorandum pad to her, and wrote on it: "Cora Felton is on the line. She seems very much worked up and would like to have you talk with her. She knows that Mrs. Winters is here."

She passed the message across the desk to Mason. He read it, nodded to her, picked up his own telephone, and said, "Gertie, connect me with that call on Della's desk. . . . Hello."

"Oh, hello, Mr. Mason." Cora Felton's voice was apologetic. "I'm terribly sorry to bother you. I suppose this is a pretty small matter for a man of your standing, but since you already know about the case and have had a sort of unofficial connection with it, I thought . . . Well, Mr. Mason, I don't know how much we are going to make out of

21

it—how much Eva is going to, I mean—but would it cost an awful lot to have you investigate it, at least to the point of making sure that Eva is not doing anything illegal?"

"I presume that could be arranged," Mason replied, "as far as the financial details are concerned."

"Oh, Mr. Mason, I'd be *so* relieved if you would take an interest in it. I have a great deal of confidence in Aunt Adelle's ability to take care of herself, but I think that the situation may be sufficiently out of the usual so that perhaps the police should be notified. Though I don't want to do that except as a last resort. Could you look into it at least enough to decide whether the police ought to be notified? And about how much would that cost?"

"The charge will be nominal," Mason said. "Am I at liberty to tell the party you mentioned about this call?"

"You mean Aunt Adelle?"

"Yes."

"Oh, I wish you would, Mr. Mason. She's worried and—"

"It's all right," Mason said. "I'll explain the situation to her. If you'll give me your number, I'll call back and let you know."

Mason scribbled the number on a pad, hung up the telephone, and turned to Adelle Winters. "That was Cora Felton on the line. She has asked me to make an investigation. Well, I'll have to talk with this man Hines. Now follow my instructions very carefully. Go back to the apartment. Don't tell Hines you have been here—let him think that you went right home in the taxi. Is it waiting down on the street, or did you discharge it?"

"No, it's waiting. You see, I thought perhaps Mr. Hines might be there by the time I arrived, and if he saw me show up with another cab driver . . ."

"Good!" Mason commented. "Now you go on back there. Go up to the apartment. Start living just the same as usual. In about an hour I'll telephone. I'll tell you that I'm Perry Mason, the attorney, and I want to talk with Miss

Reedley. I'll say that I'm coming out in fifteen minutes to see Miss Reedley, that I won't take no for an answer, and that if I don't see her I'll call the police. You can then ring up Hines at the number he gave you and tell him of the conversation and ask him what you are to do about it. You won't let on you know me or that you have any idea why I'm calling."

"You think Mr. Hines will be there when you arrive?" she asked.

"He'll either be there," Mason said, "or he'll be hightailing it out of the country, depending on what sort of flim-flam he's working."

"Well," she said, "*that's* a load off my mind. I don't mind telling you, Mr. Mason, that it takes a good deal to get me worried. I've been in some pretty tight spots. But there's something about this—that sinister feeling in the place . . . You just *feel* as though somebody had been killed there. It give you the creeps. . . ."

"One more thing," Mason said. "Has there been any man in the picture? Have you been ordered to see any man, or to be seen with any man?"

"Only Mr. Hines. He has taken us to dinner with him every night since we've been there."

"Where?"

"Small restaurants—nice places, but rather small."

"Made any passes?"

"No. Of course not. I've got a gun in that purse, Mr. Mason—and I can use it. If he gets fresh with Eva, I'll pin his ears back. If he gets rough, I'll let him look at the business end of that gun as a little reminder."

"Do you have a permit to carry the gun?"

"No."

"You'd better get rid of it then. You'll get into trouble with it and be in a spot."

"Don't worry about me. I'll take care of myself. You see that Eva doesn't get into any trouble, and let me worry about my affairs. I can get by all right."

"Better either get a permit for that gun or get rid of it. And don't do anything more on the job until I get there. Just go back and sit still."

"Very well."

"All right. Remember, I'll call in an hour. Go on out and do just as I told you."

3

It was twenty minutes of twelve when Mason climbed the steps to the lobby of the apartment house and pressed the button opposite the card bearing the name Helen Reedley.

Almost at once the sound of a buzzer indicated that the catch had been thrown on the outer door. Mason pushed it open, entered the lobby, found the automatic elevator, and went up to the third floor. He strode down the corridor, found the apartment he wanted, and tapped peremptorily on the panel.

Almost immediately the door was thrown open. A man bowed affably and extended a hand—the same man who had given Cora Felton the ten dollars. "Mr. Mason, I'm very pleased to meet you. Perry Mason, the famous attorney. This is indeed a pleasure. Won't you come in?"

"I wanted to see Miss Reedley," Mason said as he started to walk through the dim foyer.

"Unfortunately, Miss Reedley has a very severe headache, and—" the man said, and stopped abruptly. "Oh . . . oh!"

As Mason entered the room the light had fallen on his face and the man had recognized him. There was consternation in the blue eyes bulging behind nose-pincher glasses that left two angry red spots where they dug into the high bridge of a prominent nose.

"Mr. Mason!" the man exclaimed. "I didn't know that you were . . . we've met before."

"I've *seen* you before," Mason said.

"When I was paying off one of the unsuccessful applicants for the job."

"That's right."

The man rubbed his finger tips along the angle of his jaw. "That complicates the situation," he said slowly.

"In what way?"

"Well . . . I'd like to know what your connection with it is."

"And *I* want to know," Mason rejoined, "what *your* connection with it is! What's your name?"

"I . . . I am Mr. Hines's representative."

"Are you Mr. Hines himself?"

"Well . . . let's say I'm his representative."

"I'm asking you for your name."

"Well, if it's important, call me—Robert Dover Hines."

"It is important," Mason said. "Sit down. Where's Helen Reedley?"

"I told you she had a severe headache."

"That doesn't conform with the facts of the case as I understand them. Now, let's quit beating around the bush. What's the game?"

"My dear Mr. Mason, I assure you that . . . Will you please tell me what *your* interest in the matter is?"

Mason said, "I want to talk with Helen Reedley."

"That is impossible at the moment."

"Nothing is impossible. That phone's connected, isn't it?"

"Yes, but I fail to see what that has to do with it."

"My own information," Mason said grimly, "is that Miss Reedley *is* available. I want to talk with her, personally, *now*. I want her to identify herself to me as the person she claims to be. In the event that she doesn't do that, I'm going to go over to that phone and notify the police."

"What are you going to notify them about?" Hines asked suavely.

"You'll find out when you hear me talk." Mason's tone was curt. "If you're curious, just say the word and you can start listening."

Hines placed his thumb on one side of his chin, the tips of his fingers on the other and made gentle, V-shaped, stroking motions. "This is indeed most unfortunate, Mr. Mason." He was still suave.

"For whom?"

"For all concerned."

"*I'm* concerned," Mason said, "and I don't think it's at all unfortunate."

"May I ask how you learned where to find this apartment?"

"Ask anything you damn please," Mason said. "If I feel like anwering, I'll answer. If I don't, I won't. In the meantime, where's Helen Reedley?"

"Mr. Mason, let's not get worked up over this—let's discuss it like practical men. Perhaps, after all, there's a chance for us to get together. I feel that it you would only be frank and tell me . . ."

Mason moved quickly across the apartment to a closed door and jerked it open. It led into a closet.

Hines rushed over toward the lawyer. "Now, Mr. Mason, Mr. Mason," he said. "You have no right to search this apartment! I must insist that you . . ."

Mason brushed him aside, jerked open another door.

This one opened into a bedroom, and in that bedroom sat Adelle Winters, her hands folded in her lap, a triumphant smile on her face. Seated near her was a brunette who was quite similar in build and general appearance to Cora Felton and who seemed definitely apprehensive.

Perry Mason bowed. "Miss Reedley?"

Hines, at his elbow, answered the question. "*That* is Miss Reedley."

"How's your headache?" Mason asked.

"I . . . I . . ."

"Come, come," Hines protested. "This highhanded procedure is entirely illegal, Mr. Mason."

"There's the phone," Mason said. "Call the police. Have me arrested."

"Come, come, Mr. Mason," Hines exclaimed again. "Let's be reasonable!"

"Suits me," Mason said. "It's your lead. Make a play and I'll follow suit."

"Well, let's go in the other room and sit down."

"The ladies, I take it, will join us?"

The woman who Mason surmised was Eva Martell glanced uneasily at Hines, but Adelle Winters was on her feet at once. "Come, dear," she said, and then added, "I presume this is the Mr. Mason who called up about an hour ago."

"The same," Mason said.

"Now, if you don't mind, I'll do the talking," Hines interposed hastily.

"I do mind," Mason retorted.

"I mean, as far as the women are concerned."

"Let's quit beating around the bush, Hines. You put an ad in a paper that has a large circulation among actresses, an ad asking for women of a certain type who were free to accept a very mysterious employment. You had them all dress alike and you spotted them on street corners. You finally picked out this young woman, probably because she most resembles the woman you want her to impersonate. Now, I've been asked to look into this thing, at least to the extent of assuring myself there's nothing illegal about it."

"Who asked you to do that?"

"A client."

Hines was evidently growing uneasy. "Mr. Mason, that answer is not satisfactory."

"It's satisfactory to me."

"You want to find out whether this thing you call an impersonation is legal or not?"

"That's right."

"Suppose I can convince you that it *is* legal?"

"Then that's all there is to it. If this young lady wants to earn money in a legal occupation, it's quite all right with me."

"Mr. Mason, I . . . Where can we talk privately?"

"Right here."

"I said *privately*."

"That's as private as you can talk."

"Well, let's sit down," Hines said reluctantly. "Let's
. . . This has taken me completely by surprise. I need a
few moments to adjust myself."

Eva Martell and Adelle Winters had seated themselves on
the davenport, Mason now took the overstuffed chair
opposite, and Hines, after some hesitation, moved up a
straight-backed chair and sat down at the table. "Mr.
Mason," he said, "I have decided to be frank with you."

"That's fine. But before you do that, let's see that we're
all square with the board. Have you paid these women what
you promised them?"

"Not yet."

"Pay them now, then."

"I will gladly pay them, but I don't like to have the
suggestion come from you or in that tone of voice."

"Pay them and there'll be no need for any suggestion."

"You have already made the suggestion."

"All right, then—damn it, pay them!"

Hines flushed. "Are they your clients?"

"In a way. A friend of theirs has asked me to keep an eye
on the situation."

After a moment of hesitation Hines took out a wallet that
was well padded with money. From it he took five fifty-
dollar bills and handed them to Eva Martell; then a hundred-
dollar bill and gave it to Adelle Winters.

"That's better," Mason said, as Hines returned the wallet
to his pocket. "Now you can start talking."

"This young woman is Miss Eva Martell," Hines began.
"The lady with her is Mrs. Adelle Winters, who acts as her
chaperone. If you saw the ad, you will recall its stipulation
that I would pay a chaperone and pay her well. For my own
protection, as well as for that of the young woman, I want to
make absolutely sure that there is nothing untoward in the

situation, nothing that could possibly lead to a . . . er
. . . morals charge."

"Okay," Mason said, "we'll assume that's taken care of.
So this is Miss Martell. Now I believe you are living here,
posing as Helen Reedley?"

"Yes," the brunette said.

"Why?"

"Because I was told to do so."

"By whom?"

She hesitated, and Adelle Winters replied. "Those were
the instructions given by Mr. Hines, this gentleman sitting
here. That's what he told us to do when we moved in.
We've followed them to the letter. Everything we've done
has been just what he told us to do."

"That right?" Mason asked.

Hines cleared his throat. "It's substantially correct," he
admitted reluctantly.

Mason said, "I take it, then, that you're willing to
assume the responsibility?"

"Entirely, sir. Every bit of it."

"And I take it you're aware it's a crime to impersonate
others?"

"Only when there is an intent to defraud, Mr. Mason. I
have looked up the law very, very carefully. I can assure you
that every step I have taken is strictly within the law. There
is no intent to defraud anyone," Hines explained.

"But you do intend to deceive people."

"There's a legal distinction."

"I know there is," Mason said. "I'm trying to find out
whether you are aware of that distincton."

"I am!"

"Who rents this apartment?"

"I . . . er . . ."

"Come on," Mason said. "Who rents it?"

"Helen Reedley."

"The real Helen Reedley?"

"Yes."

"Who gave you permission to install these two women here?"

"Well . . . I have her authorization."

"In writing?"

"No."

"There you are," Mason said.

"Look here, Mr. Mason. Let me make you a fair business proposition. Suppose I have Helen Reedley herself come to you and tell you that I represent her, that everything I am doing is all right, that there is no intention to defraud anyone, and that we will jointly assume responsibility for everything this young woman is asked to do. Suppose I do all that?"

"The real Helen Reedley?" Mason countered.

"That's right."

Mason grinned. "Number Two on your list of brunettes, I suppose?"

"Mr. Mason, Helen Reedley will have her driver's license. It will have her thumbprint on it. You will take the thumbprint directly from her hand and compare the two. Nothing could be fairer than that."

"When will this take place?"

Hines looked at his watch. "It is now approximately twelve o'clock noon. I can have her at your office at one o'clock."

"Have her there." Mason got to his feet and started for the door. At the doorway he turned and said to Eva Martell, "My number's listed in the telephone book. If there's anything you want to know about, ring me. I'll call you some time this afternoon. Until you hear from me, don't do anything."

"But Mr. Mason," Hines protested, "I assure you it's all right—all perfectly legitimate! It's . . . Hang it, you've embarrassed me by injecting your personality into this case. But, since it's been done, I can assure you that you will be satisfied—satisfied absolutely."

"I'm a hard man to satisfy," Mason told him.

"A thumbprint will satisfy you, won't it?"

"Of the identify of the thumb," Mason said, and added, "and that's all."

He closed the door and left Hines sitting there with the two women.

4

Mason, in his office, looked at his watch for the second time within ten minutes. "Well, I guess it's a stand-up," he said.

Della Street nodded.

"We'll give her another five minutes."

"You really thought she'd come?" Della Street asked.

"I didn't know. I was trying to keep an open mind."

"How did Hines impress you?"

"Not too well."

"But he's in such a vulnerable position," Della Street said. "I can't understand why he'd promise you he'd do something like that and then not do it. Unless, of course, he's just sparring for time."

"He was sparring for time all right," Mason said. "But it seems to me he could have resorted to something that would have been a little less spectacular when it failed. And he certainly could have shaded the time limit quite a bit. He could have said that he'd have her here at four o'clock and gained a cool three hours."

"And if Helen Reedley *does* show up, and her thumbprint corresponds with the one on the driving license, will you be convinced that it's all right?"

Mason laughed. "When and if she convinces me that she's the one who has the lease to that apartment and that she owns the things that are in it. After all, there may be two or three Helen Reedleys in the country. I'm never going to be really satisfied until I know exactly *why* Hines wanted to borrow a brunette to live in Helen Reedley's apartment.—

Okay, Della, here's Hines's number. Get him on the phone for me."

Della Street relayed the call through Gertie and a few moments later nodded to Mason. "He's on the line, Chief."

"Hello, Hines?" Mason said.

"Yes. Mr. Mason?"

"Right. Your party hasn't shown up yet."

"Hasn't shown up *yet!*" Hines exclaimed in a tone of utter incredulity.

"You heard me."

"I can't understand it. Why, I understood she'd be there in . . . Why, she should have been there at least twenty minutes ago."

"That was my understanding."

"I'm sure that if you'll just be patient she'll be there any minute now. She must have been detained by something unexpected."

"Let's not have any misunderstanding about this thing," Mason said. "Did you talk with her?"

"Why, yes."

"In person or over the phone?"

"Over the phone."

"And you're certain of the identity of the person with whom you talked?"

"Absolutely."

"I'll tell you what I'll do, Hines: I'll give you exactly ten minutes more. At the end of that ten minutes, my clients go out of that apartment—and, as far as they're concerned, the job's over until I know what it's all about."

"Mr. Mason, please don't do that. I simply can't afford to have them leave that apartment now. It would be . . . it would be disastrous!"

"Then get the Reedley woman in here within ten minutes," Mason said and hung up.

He noted the time. "Now," he said to Della, "have Gertie get Adelle Winters on the line. Tell her to rush the call through because Hines will probably be calling them, putting up some sort of stall."

Della Street gave the number to Gertie, telling her to rush it. Then, while she was waiting on the line, she asked, "Do you want Adelle Winters or Eva Martell?"

"Eva Martell. She's the one I'm retained to protect."

Della nodded, then suddenly turned to the telephone. "Hello. This is Mr. Mason's office. Is this— Oh, yes, Mrs. Winters, is Miss Martell there? This is Mr. Mason's office. . . . Just a minute. Mr. Mason wants to talk with you, Miss Martell."

She nodded to Perry Mason. "She's on the line. Gertie has your lined plugged in."

"Miss Martell?" Mason asked, picking up his receiver.

"Yes."

"Perry Mason talking. Hines has stood me up on that promise he made. Now, I want you to follow certain instructions to the letter."

"Yes, Mr. Mason."

"Get Mrs. Winters to accompany you. Take such clothes as you have there and have her get all the clothes she brought. Wrap them up in a package somehow, and get out."

"She has quite a few clothes, Mr. Mason. There are some suitcases here. Could we borrow one, and then—"

"Definitely not," Mason said. "I don't want anyone to have it in his or her power to trap you. Do you understand?"

"Not exactly."

"If you take so much as a penpoint out of that apartment, the real owner can claim that your original entry was felonious and that when you took her personal property from that apartment you were guilty of larceny following an unlawful entry. That's burglary, and it's a serious offense. Get what I mean?"

"Oh, yes, I see. Do you think someone *might* claim that?"

"I don't know, but I don't want to take any chances.

35

Wrap your things up in a bundle. Never mind what it looks like. Never mind what anyone says to you. Get your things together and get out."

"Mr. Mason?"

"Yes."

"Does Mr. H. know we're leaving?"

"I told him that you were going to."

"Then he'll probably come dashing over here?"

"Yes."

"He may make some promises."

"Never mind what he says," Mason told her. "You folks get out, just as I told you."

"And then what?"

"And then telephone me that you're out. That will let me know I have a free hand. Now, be sure not to take anything from that apartment. Not so much as a paper match folder."

"Where shall we go?"

"Any place. To your apartment, or to a movie—only get out, *fast*."

"Very well. We'll be out within thirty minutes."

"Make it fifteen," Mason said, and hung up to return to his dictating.

Some little time later the phone rang, and Della Street announced that Eva Martell was on the line.

"Hello, Eva. Where are you?"

"At a pay station in the Lorenzo Hotel."

"No trouble about getting out?"

"Well, he rang up. He said he was going to come to the apartment, but he didn't."

"What did he want?"

"Wanted us to stay—made us all sorts of offers. Then asked us to stay at least until he could get up and talk with us. But, Mr. Mason, the reason we're not home is that— well, we're being followed!"

"By whom?"

"Two men that we're sure of. There may be others—we don't know."

"I was afraid of that," Mason told her. "Now, you're absolutely positive that you haven't taken a single thing from that apartment that didn't belong to you?"

"Not so much as a cigarette."

"And you're sure these men are following you?"

"Yes."

"Do they know that you know it?"

"I don't think so. We wouldn't have noticed them if it hadn't been that we were . . . well, you know, sort of watching, a little nervous."

"Hines didn't come up?"

"No. We got out at one forty-five. I noticed the time, just in case it should be necessary to tell *exactly* when we left. Aunt Adelle was a little slow or we'd have been out before. She had some phoning to do, and I made her do it from the lobby. She tried to get you but the line was busy, and no one answered at the Hines number. It's the first time that's happened; he told us there'd *always* be someone at that number day and night. Once before when we called and he wasn't there a woman answered. We're wondering, since what he said to you, whether that woman might have been the real Helen Reedley. That is, I suggested it to Aunt Adelle. You know what *she* thinks—*she* says Helen Reedley is dead, and—"

"What did Hines say over the phone?"

"He was awfully excited. Said you're unreasonable; that we're not doing anything wrong, and that, after all, the party that was to see you had another engagement. He said that if you'd only been patient for a short time she'd have been there and given you a complete release and everything would have been all right."

"Talk is cheap," Mason said. "I'll ring up and tell him that whenever he can satisfy me you girls will go back, but that in the meantime you have walked out because he was asking you to do something that was illegal; that, as far as we're concerned, you're still entitled to compensation. We'll expect him to come through."

"He made all sorts of promises," Eva said. "One thing that he *did* do, Mr. Mason—he asked us particularly not to go home until after five o'clock. He said that if we'd go to some public place and wait, by five o'clock everything would be all right and we could come back; but that if we ever went to our own apartment, the whole thing was off."

"Did he say why?"

"No, but he was very emphatic about it, and that was his phrase—that if we went to our apartment, then the whole thing was off as far as he was concerned."

"And that's why you went to the Lorenzo Hotel?"

"That, and because of the people who are following us."

"I'm glad you're out," Mason told her. "I'm free to do my stuff now. Wait right there at the Lorenzo. Don't leave until you telephone me and get a clearance that it's all right. Be sure now, stay right there."

Mason received her promise, then said to Della Street, "Della, run down the hall to the Drake Detective Agency. Tell Paul Drake these two women are at the Lorenzo Hotel and that they're being shadowed. I want to find out who the shadows are and to whom they're reporting. Tell Paul to send four or five men to handle the job. I want him, first, to spot the people that are doing the shadowing, and then to get on their trail and shadow *them*. You can describe the women to Paul so that his men can pick them up without any trouble. They'll be there in the lobby of the Lorenzo. Tell him to spare no expense. A smart guy by the name of Hines is going to pay for it."

Della rushed out of the door.

Mason jiggled the receiver hook with his finger and, when his operator came in on the line, said, "Gertie, get me that apartment. You have the number out there."

"Okay."

"If they don't answer, try the Hines number, Drexberry 5236."

"Yes, Mr. Mason."

"Rush it."

"Yes, sir. You want me to call you when I—"

"No, I'll wait on the line, Gertie. Rush it as fast as you can. Get me Mr. Hines on the line."

Mason heard the whir of the telephone mechanism as her fingers dialed the number. Then he sat listening to the sound of the ringing telephone.

"There seems to be no answer, Mr. Mason, at the Reedley apartment. I'll try the Drexberry number."

Once more she dialed, and once more Mason heard the sound of the ringing telephone. Then, once again, there was a pause.

"They're just not answering," Gertie said.

Mason said, "Try them again in five minutes. And, Gertie, if Hines should ring in, I'm very anxious to talk with him. No matter what's going on be sure to put the call directly through to my office."

"Mr. Hines?"

"That's right—Robert Dover Hines."

"Okay. I'll put the calls right through."

As Mason dropped the receiver back into place he heard Della Street's quick steps in the corridor, and a moment later she was fitting her key into the exit door of his private office.

"That's fast work," Mason said.

"I was lucky enough to catch Paul Drake in the corridor just as he was leaving for the elevator. I outlined the situation to him and he's getting busy on it right away."

"I tried to get Hines, but couldn't get him," Mason said. "No one answered at the apartment. I told Gertie if he called in to rush the call right through."

"You think he'll call?"

"I don't know. I'm hoping he will. I've got my clients out of that apartment and I'm in a bargaining position now. This is going to give him a jolt."

"Why are you better off now that they are out, Chief?"

"Because we don't know a darn thing about him," replied Mason. "He could have stepped out of the picture and left the women holding the sack when the police arrived and found Eva Martell going under the name of Helen Reedley, living in Helen Reedley's apartment, wearing Helen Reedley's clothes, and . . . well, you know the answer. We'd have a lot of explaining to do."

"Do you suppose it's Hines who is having those girls shadowed?"

"It could be. Hines was very anxious that they should merely go to some public place and wait. He emphasized particularly that if they went to their own apartment, everything would be off—and may be having them shadowed now to see that they don't go there."

"But why?"

"That's what we're trying to find out."

"Do you think the real Helen Reedley is dead?"

"I don't know. She could be. As yet we haven't enough information even to speculate. But there's one fact that is very significant."

"What?"

"The instructions given to Adelle Winters. Whenever any friend of Helen Reedley called the apartment, Mrs. Winters was to stall the party, promise that Helen Reedley would call back in fifteen or twenty minutes, report to Hines—and then forget it."

"Well, wouldn't that indicate that the Reedley woman might be—Oh, I *see!* If she *didn't* call back, the friend would get suspicious."

"Exactly, Della. If Hines merely wanted to stall Helen's friends along, he would have had a better one than that—such as that Miss Reedley was out shopping, or visiting in the country, or something like that. But to say that she'd call back in fifteen or twenty minutes meant that he'd have to make good."

"How do you suppose he did that?"

"By having Helen Reedley call back, just as he'd had Adelle Winters say she would."

"But how?"

"Simple enough. Helen Reedley is afraid of something. She ducks and stays in hiding. She can't be dead, because evidently she's able to call her friends back. They, of course, have no way of knowing she isn't calling from her own apartment, and—" He was interrupted by the ringing of the telephone.

"This is probably Hines now," he said, as he picked up the telephone.

But it was Gertie's voice that came over the wire. "A Helen Reedley is out here. Says she had an appointment with you for earlier in the afternoon. She was unable to keep it and—"

"Send her in," Mason said. "Get her in here right away."

He hung up and, nodding to Della Street, said, "Helen Reedley. This is going to be good."

The door from the outer office opened and Gertie ushered in a trim young brunette. The newcomer looked at Della Street first, appraising her coolly from head to feet. Then she turned to Perry Mason. "How do you do, Mr. Mason? I'm Helen Reedley. Good of you to see me so promptly. I'm sorry I was late."

"Won't you sit down?" Mason said. "There are some questions I wanted to ask you."

"So I was given to understand."

She crossed the office with a smooth sweep of slim-waisted grace, a young woman who was quite aware that her figure would not go unnoticed. In externals she seemed an exact duplicate of Eva Martell, even to a noticeable resemblance in features. What differentiated her from Eva was the supercharged effect that she radiated. Not only were her motions smooth, with the grace that comes from perfect health, but their timing was slow, calculated, tantalizing. Her large dark eyes, with their long, sweeping lashes, moved provocatively under delicately arched brows as she glanced up at Mason, completely ignoring Della.

"What was it that you wanted to know, Mr. Mason?" she asked.

"What," Mason countered as he sized her up, "do you want to tell me?"

For a moment a shade of annoyance flashed across her features. "Mr. Hines told me you had some questions," she returned. Her voice, like her motions, had just that trick of timing which made a definite impression on the listener. And Mason noticed that at the end of every speech she raised her eyebrows slightly and at the same time tilted her face upward and to one side.

"I have only one question," he said, "and I have already asked it: What do you want to tell me?"

She frowned. "About what?"

"About anything."

"I understand you are interested in my apartment."

"It *is* your apartment?"

"Naturally."

"You have proof of that?"

"Mr. Hines *told* me you might be difficult . . . Now— may I draw my chair up a little closer? And if you'll pull out that leaf in your desk . . . Here are the documents that prove my identity."

Opening her purse she took out a folding leather wallet and from it produced a driving license. "Made out to Helen Reedley," she said. "You'll notice that the address is the same as that of the apartment in question. There's a thumbprint on the license. Now, if you'll notice my thumb, Mr. Mason . . . Perhaps you have an inked pad there for rubber stamps? Thank you. Observe, I press my thumb on the pad—and if you have a piece of paper?—There you are: my thumbprint. Please notice that it corresponds exactly with the thumbprint on the license."

Helen Reedley took some cleansing tissue from her purse, wiped her thumb free of ink, dropped the tissue in Mason's wastebasket, settled back in the chair, and waited for him to compare the thumbprint with the print on the driving license.

"It's all right to smoke?" she asked.

"Quite," Mason said without looking up from the thumbprint. Once more she showed a faint flicker of annoyance. But she took a cigarette case from her purse, extracted a cigarette from it and a lighter, lit the cigarette, and studied Mason with a sidelong glance.

"The prints appear to be identical," Mason said.

"They *are* identical."

"I notice that the address here is the address of the apartment we're talking about. But perhaps you have still other proof?"

"Certainly," she replied calmly. "I understood that you would want plenty. I have here a series of rent receipts signed by the manager of the premises. You will notice that they are for consecutive months for the past six months."

"You have a Social Security number?" Mason asked.

"No." There was comtempt in the monosyllable.

"You have other means of identification than the driving license?"

"Certainly. I have credit cards, golf-club membership cards, and various other things, but I see no reason to produce them. Certainly this driver's license vouches for my identity—it's dated six months ago."

"Better let me see some of those other cards," Mason said.

This time she was, for a moment, definitely angry. But she wordlessly produced some half-dozen cards and passed them across for inspection.

Mason pulled pencil and paper toward him and started making a list of the cards with dates and numbers.

"Really, Mr. Mason, is that necessary?"

"I think it is."

"Very well," she said in tight-lipped anger.

When Mason had finished with them, he handed them back to her.

She had waited for that moment when his hand was extended toward hers. Now she brushed his hand with the tips of her fingers as she took the cards, suddenly favoring him with a dazzling smile. "And now that we've completed the nasty part, Mr. Mason, can't we be friends?"

Mason grinned. "But we haven't completed the nasty part, yet. You own the apartment—that is, you rent it. So what?"

"My friend, Mr. Hines, is in complete charge of my affairs so far as they concern that apartment."

"And its contents?" Mason asked.

"It's contents, too."

"All of them?"

"Everything."

Mason turned to Della Street. "Take this down, will you, Della?"

"To whom it may concern:

This is to certify that the undersigned, Helen Reedley, is, and for some six months past has been, the tenant of an apartment in that certain apartment house known as the Siglet Manor situate on Eighth Street, and specifically, the number of the apartment so rented by the undersigned being designated as number 326 in said apartment house. I represent, warrant, and state that I am the sole owner of all property in said apartment; that one Robert Dover Hines is my agent and attorney in fact for the purpose of dealing with said apartment and with all of the contents thereof; that he may, at his discretion, permit any person or persons to enter into said apartment, to remain there as long as the said Hines desires, and on such terms as he may care to make; that such person or persons, with the consent of the said Robert Dover Hines, may use, take, convert, transport, or otherwise dispose of any or all of the contents of said apartment including my own personal wearing apparel, toilet articles, and accessories, or any other thing of any sort, nature, or description which may be situate in said apartment. I herby ratify everything the said Robert Dover Hines has done in connection with such matters and agree to abide by any agreement he may make in connection with such apartment."

"Put a blank for a signature on that, Della, and then bring your notarial seal. You can put an acknowledgment on it."

"I say," Helen Reedley protested, "isn't that going rather strong?"

Mason met her eyes, smiled, and said, "Yes."

As Della Street withdrew to type the document, Mason lit a cigarette and settled back in the chair. "Now the 'nasty part' is over, and we can be friends."

Her eyes were blazing with anger. "But now I don't *want* to be friends!"

Mason smiled. "You know, of course, what Hines is doing?"

"Certainly."

"And what," Mason asked, "is the reason for all this?"

"That's purely personal."

"I'll have to know."

"That document I'm going to sign protects you."

"It affords us adequate protection *provided* I know the reason for what is going on."

"I see no reason to tell you."

"In the event you don't," Mason said, "it's going to be necessary to strengthen that document."

"If you find any way of strengthening that, I'll eat it!"

Mason pushed the button on his desk. When Della Street appeared from the adjoining office he said, "Get your book, Della. I'm going to put some additional stuff in that release."

Helen Reedley sat in tight-lipped angry silence.

Della Street returned with her notebook, settled herself in

the secretarial chair by Mason's desk, and held her pencil poised.

"I further understand [Mason dictated] that the said Robert Dover Hines has installed certain parties in the said apartment, one of whom has been instructed by the said Hines to use the name of Helen Reedley. I hereby consent to the use of my name, the signing of my said name, or the impersonation of me by such person at such times and in such manner and for such purposes as my agent, the said Robert Dover Hines, may instruct, and I hereby waive any claim of any sort, nature, or description against said person, because, or by reason of, her use of my said name, and agree to hold her harmless for any damages which may be suffered because of so impersonating me and fully indemnify her against any financial loss of any sort, nature, or description incurred through following the instruction of my said agent, Robert Dover Hines."

There was a sudden crash as Helen Reedley jumped indignantly to her feet; her purse slipped from her lap and fell to the floor, spilling some of its contents over the office carpet. "Do you think I'll sign any such thing as that?" she blazed. "That's absolutely beyond all reason. It's impertinent, it's . . . it's . . . suicidal!"

Suavely Mason broke in on her sputtering indignation. "I suggested to you, Miss Reedley, that it might be much better to confide in me fully and tell me the purpose back of all this. I told you that if you didn't I'd strengthen that document."

"But that's absurd—absolutely ridiculous! Why, under that document the girl could go to my bank and sign my name to a check for five thousand dollars and calmly walk off thumbing her nose at me."

"She certainly could," Mason said, "*provided*, of

course, that your agent, Mr. Hines, told her she could do so."

"Well, Hines isn't my agent to *that* extent."

"Then you'd better tell me a little more about Mr. Hines and the extent to which he *is* your agent."

"I've told you everything I intend to."

"I'm sorry," Mason said. "Either I get that information, or I get a signature to that document. Go ahead and type it up, Della.—You'd better pick up your things there on the floor, Miss Reedley. And incidentally, if you're carrying a gun in that purse, you should have a permit."

"How do you know I haven't one?" she flared.

"I don't," Mason said. "But if you do have, by all means let me see it because that in itself will be a means of identification."

She bent angrily over her purse, pushed the things back into it, snapped the purse shut, and got to her feet. "God, how I hate men like you!" she exclaimed.

"The men you like are the ones you can twist around your thumb. I'm not exactly immune, Miss Reedley, but I've always made it a rule never to let an attractive woman influence me in my protection of my clients' interests."

"I'll say you haven't!" she blazed.

"Now then," Mason said, "do you tell me what it's all about, or do you sign that agreement?"

"As far as I'm concerned, you can—" She stopped abruptly in mid-sentence.

"Well?" Mason asked.

She took a deep breath, then seemed to relax. "I'll be only to glad to sign it. Have your secretary type it up at once, will you please, because I'm in a hurry."

Mason said, "One thing about you when you yield, you yield with good grace!"

Her quiet smile was enigmatical.

"And now," Mason said, "we can start being friends."

"Now," she said, "I've changed my mind."

And she sat in frigid silence until Della Street brought in

the document together with a fountain pen, an acknowledgment blank, and her notarial seal.

Mason checked the document and passed it over to Helen
Reedley for her signature.

Helen Reedley all but snatched the pen that Della Street
was holding, glanced through the document hastily, and
affixed a scrawled signature.

Mason extended the inked pad. "And if you don't
mind," he said, "the thumbprint."

She slammed her thumb down on the inked pad and
banged it on the paper, groped for a cleansing tissue, failed
to find one, brought out an expensive handkerchief, and
smeared the ink from her thumb all over the handkerchief.

"Do you," Della Street asked, "solemnly acknowledge
that you are Helen Reedley, that you have signed this
document, and that it is your free and voluntary act?"

"Yes! And now let me get the hell out of here before I
smash something."

Mason said calmly, "Miss Street, will you please show
Miss Reedley the way out?"

Della Street very deliberately stamped her notarial acknowledgment on the certificate over her signature, moved
over to the exit door and held it open. Helen Reedley, her
head high, swept through.

"Good afternoon, Miss Reedley," Della said.

There was no answer.

Della waited until the automatic door-check had clicked
the door shut. Then she came back to Mason's desk. "Gosh,
Chief, did you see the way she looked me over?"

"I did," Mason said. "And it was just because of that
look that I may have been a little harsher with her than I
would otherwise have been."

"Forget it!" laughed Della. "It's just the way one woman
looks over another. I don't think your brunette friend would
take kindly to any competition. Was that a gun she was
carrying in her purse?"

"Darned if I know. There was *something* heavy and solid

in there. When the purse hit the carpet, it hit with quite a thud. Some of the lighter stuff spilled out, but the heavy thing, whatever it was, stayed inside. I tried to draw her out to see if she would admit it was a gun, but she wouldn't."

"I'd hate to have *that* woman looking for me with a gun," said Della.

"I'm not certain but that—"

The telephone interrupted him, and he nodded to Della.

She picked up the instrument. "Yes—hello. . . . Yes, Gertie, I'll tell him." She turned to Mason. "Eva Martell on the line wanting to know if there have been any new developments."

"I'll talk with her," Mason said.—"Hello, Eva. Helen Reedley has been here. She's just left the office. I think there's no doubt that she *is* the Helen Reedley who owns that apartment and presumably the owner of the things in it. At any rate, the document she signed will put you folks in the clear provided you follow Hines's instructions. I've been trying to get him on the phone but haven't been able to locate him. Are you to go right back?"

"Yes," Eva Martell said. "He told us that just as soon as we got an okay from you we were to go right back to the Reedley apartment and pick up where we'd left off. Gosh, though, we'd like to do some shopping."

"Go ahead and do your shopping if you want to. But remember you're being shadowed. Remember, too, that Hines has said you mayn't go to your own apartment."

"Yes, I know. But there are some things in the window of a department store near here that have been very hard to get. Suppose—Well, could you pretend to Mr. Hines that you had trouble reaching us? That there was some delay? We'd like to—"

Mason laughed. "Go right ahead. I think Hines is so anxious to keep you that he'd put up with almost anything. Otherwise, Helen Reedley would never have consented to all those terms I laid down."

"Thank you, Mr. Mason. I suppose you have her authorization in writing?"

"In writing," Mason said, "acknowledged before a notary and stamped with her thumbprint."

Eva Martell laughed. "Well, I guess that should do the job."

"I hope so. Are the men still on your trail?"

"Yes. And some other men just came in. They are looking us over, and—"

"Don't pay any attention to them," Mason said. "Go about your business just as though you had no idea you were being followed. Then get a taxi, go back to the Reedley apartment, and resume housekeeping. You have nothing to worry about."

"Gosh, Mr. Mason, you've taken a load off my mind. What did Helen Reedley look like? Anything like me?"

"Very much like you, so far as physical characteristics are concerned."

"How about temperament?"

"It's not temperament, it's temperature!"

"Well, I hope I'm not ice cold."

Mason laughed. "I saw Helen Reedley under circumstances that encouraged a rise in temperature."

"Is she prettier than I am?"

"She's definitely not in the same class with you," Mason said.

"Well . . . thanks. I was wondering . . . I've noticed Mr. Hines looking me over—and, well, you know . . . Thank you, Mr. Mason."

"You mean you're falling for Hines?"

"No, no, nothing like that. Definitely not. Only one can't help wondering, in the circumstances. But I mustn't keep you. Good-by, Mr. Mason—and thank you again."

5

It was around six-thirty when Mason, who had been working late at the office, heard the persistent buzzing of the switchboard in the outer office and said to Della Street, "Perhaps you'd better answer it, Della. It may be Eva Martell. We have a dinner date with Paul Drake at seven o'clock, so we won't have time to see anyone."

Della Street nodded and went out to the switchboard. She came hurrying back. "It's Eva Martell, Chief. She says she has to talk with you right away. I've plugged her in on your line if you want to talk with her."

Mason picked up the phone. "Hello, Eva. Where are you now, at the apartment?"

The voice that came over the line was almost hysterical with excitement. "Mr. Mason, you'll have to tell us what to do. We're back at the apartment. Something has happened! We'd like to have you over here right away."

"I'm just getting ready to leave here," Mason said, "but I have a dinner date in twenty minutes. What seems to be the trouble?"

"I don't want to tell you over the phone. I'd like to have you come over right away if you could."

"Something serious?" Mason asked.

"Something *quite* serious, I'm afraid."

Mason glanced at his watch and frowned. "I'm terribly busy," he said. "Why not tell me now? That telephone at the Reedley apartment doesn't go through any downstairs switchboard, and the document that has just been signed protects you on just about anything that can happen. Tell me what's worrying you."

51

"It's Robert Hines," Eva replied, her tone charged with excitement. "He's sitting in a chair here in the apartment, and there's what looks like a bullet hole in the middle of his forehead. He's dead—I'm sure of it!"

"What the *devil!* How long has he been there?"

"I don't know."

"When was he shot?"

"I don't know that either—I don't know a thing about it."

"Have you called the police?"

"No—just you."

"How long have you been there at the apartment?"

"We just got here. After you told us we could go shopping . . . well, it took longer than we had planned. After all—"

"Notify the police—right now," Mason told her. "And don't try to cover up anything. I'll be doing things here." He slammed down the receiver, dashed out through the door, and ran down the corridor to the offices of the Drake Detective Agency, jerked open the door and called out to the girl at the desk, "Paul Drake in?"

She nodded, pointing toward Drake's private office, and at the same time pressed a button releasing the electric lock on the gateway that separated the offices from the reception room.

Mason rushed down the passage and burst in on Drake in his private office.

Drake looked up from some reports he was checking. "Hello, Perry. What's the rush? Twenty minutes yet before—"

"That job I gave you out at the Lorenzo Hotel—you got some good men on it?"

"Three of them. The best in the business."

"Okay. Paul, get this—it's important. A man by the name of Hines was bumped off at the Siglet Manor Apartments. That's out on Eighth Street. Apartment three twenty-six."

"Who discovered the murder?"

"My clients—the ones who are being tailed by the men I wanted your operatives to spot. The call is going in to the police right now. They'll get in touch with a radio car. We probably have approximately three minutes."

"Oh-oh," Drake said.

"Now then," Mason went on, "I realize as well as you do that these men we're shadowing are probably private detectives. We'll have no difficulty trailing them to the office of some detective agency. But the trail will stop right there. Barring some lucky break, we won't be able to find who employed the detectives. Reports will be sent to the client by mail, and we'll be left butting our heads against a brick wall."

"I'm glad you understand that, Perry, because if these men are private detectives, that's exactly what we're going to be up against."

"Okay. Now, here's a break. Within a matter of minutes the police will come boiling into the Siglet Manor. My clients have gone there, which means that the men who are trailing them have also gone there. They'll see the police come in and know something has happened, but they won't know what it is. It'll take them a while to find out."

"Not very long," Drake said. "If those fellows are any good, they'll have ways of getting information out of the police."

"Don't I know it! Now, what'll happen when they do?"

"What do you mean?"

"Put yourself in their position. Suppose *your* agency were handling the thing, and you ran slap-bang into a murder—what would you do?"

"In the first place, my operatives would rush the information to me—either personally or by telephone. I'd immediately get in touch with my client and advise him and ask for instructions."

"How would you get in touch with your client?"

"Probably by telephone."

"How much could you tell him over the telephone?"

"Just the high spots."

"What would the client do?"

"You mean," Drake asked, "would he come rushing into the agency and be closeted with me, getting information hot off the bat?"

"That's right."

Drake nodded. "You've got something there, Perry."

"Okay. How long will it take you to cover that angle?"

"Not very long. If one of those operatives phones his agency, one of my men may get close enough to the booth to see what number he's dialing. If he goes to report in person, he'll be tailed."

"Okay," Mason said. "Now then, let's act on the assumption that the trail will lead to a private detective agency. I want enough men on the job to shadow that agency, and if anyone comes in who looks as though he's in a hurry on a matter of some urgency, I want that man shadowed when he leaves the agency."

"Okay," Drake said. "It won't take more than two men in addition to the ones we have."

"All right. Get them."

"Any chance your clients had anything to do with the murder?" Drake asked.

"Don't be silly, Paul. My clients *never* have anything to do with murders. These people simply happened to stumble over the corpse. They notified me and wanted me to come out. I have already used up my allotment of corpse-discoveries so far as the police are concerned. I told them to get in touch with the police."

"And tell them they're your clients?"

"Why not?"

"That's going to make for a lot of interesting developments. . . . I'll put these calls through, get my men on the job, and then come down to your office."

"Before you leave here," Mason said, "try to get all the details that are available about the killing."

"You say Hines was the victim?"

"That's right."

"And he's the one who hired the women?"

"Right."

"Well, let me put these calls through, Perry, and get the men on the job. Maybe we'll find out something." And Drake was reaching for the telephone as Mason left the office.

"Did you get Paul all right?" Della Street asked when he had returned to his desk.

Mason nodded. "Paul Drake's going to have men on the job covering the whole thing. He'll also get details about the murder. Meantime, there's nothing much to do except stick around and bite our fingernails. I'd give a good deal to be there right now. That's the trouble: I've too often been on the ground when corpses have been discovered. This time I'll keep in the *back*ground."

"How long do you suppose we'll have to wait?"

"For detailed information?"

"Yes."

"It depends."

"On what?"

"Several things. The breaks, mostly. If one of the persons shadowing those women gets in touch with his principal personally, and *if* we get the breaks, we *could* know something within an hour."

Della Street thought things over for a while. "Gosh," she said, "there's one thing that keeps cropping up in my mind."

"What's that?"

"Adelle Winters having a .32-caliber revolver in her handbag. Do you suppose the police will search her?"

"You're reading my mind!" Mason said.

"If it turns out that Mr. Hines has been shot by a .32 gun," Della went on reflectively, "wouldn't that . . . What *would* it do?"

"That depends. It might not mean too much. Of course, the whole thing will depend on what happens when they recover the bullet and the ballistics experts get done with it. They can tell whether it was or was not fired from any particular gun. You know that."

"*If* they have the bullet?"

"That's right."

Della was looking at Mason in a peculiar way. "And the gun?"

"And the gun."

"That last," she said slowly, "changes the situation."

"No, it doesn't change it any," Mason returned, "but it does complicate it."

"Of course, no one knows just how smart Adelle Winters is."

Mason grinned and looked at his watch. "We'll probably have an answer to that question, too, within an hour, Della. Lets go get something to eat."

6

It was after nine o'clock and Mason was pacing the floor when Paul Drake's peculiarly spaced code knock sounded on the door of the outer office.

"That's Paul," Mason said. "Let him in, will you, Della."

As Drake entered the office he said, "Hi, Della!" and, with a grimace at Mason, blew out his breath in a weary whistle. "Gosh, Perry, I've been busy!"

"Found out anything?"

"I think we've struck pay dirt."

"Shoot."

Drake dropped sidewise into the big overstuffed leather chair. "Your two women did a lot of shopping. Then they had dinner and went back to the apartment. My boys had spotted the chaps who were shadowing them and had no difficulty in trailing along behind."

"The men who were shadowing the women followed them in their shopping and to the apartment?"

"That's right."

"And your men shadowed the shadows?"

"Right."

"Then what?"

"Then all hell broke loose. Sirens, police cars, and excitement. Thanks to your tip, I got some reinforcements there in time and we were able to cover everything."

"Just what happened?"

"Well, one of the chaps rushed out to a public telephone. My operative had a small, very powerful pair of binoculars and he was able to look through the glass door of the booth and get the number the man dialed. He looked it up, and it's the number of the Interstate Investigators. My man telephoned me what he'd found out, and I immediately rushed men to the Interstate office, just as you'd instructed.

"Out at the scene of the crime, the Interstate men were busy trying to find someone they could pump, someone who knew the low-down. Finally, from a friendly police officer they got as much as anyone could get—the same as the newspaper men are getting. It may not be all the story, but it's most of it."

"Which was what?" Mason asked.

"Well, you know the identity of the corpse. What do you know about the murder itself?"

"Nothing."

"Well, Hines had been shot in the middle of the forehead with a small-caliber gun, probably a .32."

"Any wound of exit?"

"No."

"Then the bullet's still in the skull?"

"That's right."

"When the police get that, they can check the gun from which it was fired."

"Right."

"That'll simplify matters somewhat."

"Or complicate them," Drake said dryly, "depending on whether the gun was owned by your client or somebody else's client! . . . Well, the Interstate boys kept going down to the phone and feeding details into the office just as fast as they could get them. Then Interstate sent a relief man out and called in one of the men who was on the job. I figured that meant the client was coming to the office and wanted a personal report. So we had everything in readiness. Sure enough, a rather properous-looking chap of forty-two or forty-three, around five feet ten, weight about a hundred and ninety pounds, wavy red hair, pearl-gray hat, and double-breasted gray suit with a small check-plaid pattern came bustling into the office. He was in there half an hour. When he left, our men picked him up and followed him down to his car—a big, high-powered outfit. We looked up the license number later. Our men tagged him out to one of the swank apartment houses and got his name from the janitor, and by that time we'd checked up on the car license and had the same name for that."

"What's the name, Paul?"

"Orville L. Reedley," Drake said.

Mason whistled. "Any relation to Helen Reedley?"

"As soon as we got the name," Drake went on, "I had a man look up a contact in the library of one of the newspapers. After pawing through the records he found that Orville L. Reedley married Helen Honcutt in March 1942. She gave her age as twenty-one, he gave his as thirty-eight. As nearly as we can tell from the information in these statistics, it's the same Helen Reedley who has the apartment up there."

"This chap, Reedley," Mason asked, "what does he do?"

"He seems to be a broker."

Mason drummed on the edge of his desk with his finger tips. "Where is he now?"

"Still holed up in his apartment with two of my men watching the place."

Mason pushed back his chair. "Let's go, Paul," he said.

"Your car or mine?" Drake asked.

"Where's yours?"

"Right outside."

"We'll take it."

"Where do you want me?" Della Street asked.

"Right here in the office, I guess, Della. We'll get in touch with you. It may be we'll want you to take down a statement after a while. You don't mind sticking around?"

"Not a bit."

"Let's go, Paul," and the two men left.

Mason lit a cigarette as Drake started the car. "Now we're beginning to see a pattern," he said, as Drake pulled up at the first traffic signal that was against them.

"You mean the husband angle?"

"Uh-huh, and the private-detective angle."

"It has possibilities," Drake admitted.

"Of course, we're in the position of taking two and two and making four out of it, and then trying to find something to add that will give us the total of ten. But we can make a reasonable guess at the figure we want."

"How reasonable is the guess, and what's the figure?" Drake asked, grinning.

"A wife comes to a city and starts a living by herself. A husband wants to get a divorce. She'd like to have a property settlement, but her husband doesn't want to be that generous. She says, 'Okay, then we'll get along without a divorce.' He waits a while, finds that the shoe is pinching, and decides to employ some detectives to get something on her. She's running around with a boyfriend, but she's smart enough to know when the dicks are going to be put on the job. No—wait a minute, Paul! There has to be a leak somewhere. She has to know that her husband is going to employ detectives *before* he actually employs them."

"How do you figure that out?"

"Because as soon as he employed them, he'd give them her address and they'd pick her up and start following *her*. But, knowing that he's going to employ detectives, she makes arrangements to give them all a run-around. She turns the apartment over to a brunette who looks like her, and she's just as anxious as the substitute to make sure there'll be a chaperone on hand at all times. Then everything is done with the utmost propriety. The husband's detectives are probably shown a photograph that's a fuzzy snapshot, given a description, and told to go to that address, pick up Helen Reedley, and shadow her day and night. They get on the job, the address is right, the apartment is in the name of Helen Reedley. A brunette who answers the description of the woman they want is living there. They start shadowing her. There's a chaperone living there with her, and the two are inseparable. The husband gets a steady string of reports showing the greatest decorum all around. He gets discouraged and tells his lawyers to make the best settlement possible in the circumstances."

"And in the meantime the real Helen Reedley is out playing around?" Drake asked.

"Well," Mason said, "she's probably being a little discreet about things, but my guess is that she isn't spending the long evenings by the fireside with her crocheting and knitting."

"Then this man Hines must be her boy friend."

"Somehow I don't think so," Mason said. "I think she'd be too smart to let the boy friend be around the apartment, because the husband's detectives might start tailing *him*. No, I have an idea this fellow Hines is a stooge of some sort."

"*Was*," suggested Drake.

"Was is right," Mason amended.

"Well, what do you propose to do with this husband when we get there?"

"I'm going to ask questions."

"Suppose he doesn't answer them?"

"Then I'll have to guess at the answers from his manner and the way he handles himself."

"And that may be hard," Drake pointed out.

"It may be impossible," Mason conceded, "but in any event we'll have made a try. . . . Any idea what time they guy was murdered, Paul?"

"Apparently early in the afternoon. But you know how the police are, Perry. They aren't putting out too much along that line right now. They'll have the autopsy surgeons making examinations, but they won't stick their necks out with the answer until after they've found a suspect who fits into that particular schedule pretty accurately. *You* know how it is. The same way the police give out that someone has made a 'tentative identification' of a suspect—which means that they haven't a case, but aren't burning any bridges in case they can't find a better bet."

Mason nodded.

Drake piloted the car around a corner and found a parking place. "Looks like the only parking place in the block," he said. "The apartment we want is that swanky one down there about half a block."

He locked the car and put the keys in his pocket, and he and Mason walked down the sidewalk, past expensive residences, and turned in at the rather ornate front of a high-class apartment house.

The lobby had that subdued, deep-carpeted hush so frequently associated with the outward semblance of ultrarespectability. A quiet-voiced clerk on duty at the desk inquired the name of the tenant they wished to see.

"Orville Reedley," Mason replied.

"Is he expecting you?"

"Probably not. The name is Mason."

"Yes, sir—and the other gentleman's name?"

"Drake," Mason said. "Tell him I'm a lawyer."

"Oh, you're *Perry* Mason!"

"That's right."

"Yes, Mr. Mason, just a moment."

The clerk scribbled a note, pushed it through the wicket to the telephone operator, waited a few seconds, then turned and nodded to Mason. "Mr. Reedley will see you," he said. "The boy in the elevator will direct you to his apartment."

Mason and Drake entered the elevator. The boy took them to the fifth floor. "It's Apartment 5-B," he said, "the third door down on the left."

Here again in the corridor was an atmosphere of quiet seclusion. Drake turned to Mason with a grin. "It stinks of dough," he said.

Mason nodded as he pressed the mother-of-pearl button at Apartment 5-B.

The man who opened the door answered the description that had been given to Drake's operative. But, dominating the physical characteristics of age, height, weight, and complexion which would have appealed to a professional detective, was the surging, dynamic power emanating from the man even as he stood there on the threshold.

Hot, smoldering eyes regarded his two visitors. "Which one of you is Mason?"

"I am," Mason said stepping forward and extending his hand.

Reedley hesitated a moment, took the hand, but turned almost at once to Drake. "Who's the other one?"

"Paul Drake."

"What does he do?"

"He assists me in some of my cases."

"Lawyer?"

"No."

"What?"

"Detective."

Reedley thought that over, his eyes moving from one to the other. Abruptly he stepped back in the doorway and said, "Come in."

Mason and Paul Drake crossed the threshold. Reedley's powerful shoulders swung in a smooth pivot, pushing the door shut."

"Sit down."

Mason and Drake found comfortable chairs in a living room whose Venetian blinds, Oriental rugs, and comfortable, well-chosen chairs bespoke taste and wealth.

"Well," Reedley said, "what's it all about?"

"Your wife's living here in town?" Mason asked.

"What business is it of yours?"

"Frankly," Mason said, "I don't know."

"What do you mean by that?"

"It may be important in a case I am handling."

"You're a lawyer?"

"That's right."

"You have clients?"

"Exactly."

"They pay you?"

"Yes."

"You represent their interests?"

"Right."

"And only their interests?"

"Naturally."

"I am not your client. Somebody else is. Therefore you're representing somebody else. Those interests may be adverse to mine. If they are, you're my enemy. Why the hell should I answer your questions?"

"Any reason why you shouldn't?"

"I don't know."

"Could any circumstances exist that would give you any possible reason for not telling me about where your wife is living now?"

"I don't even know that. Why *should* I tell you about it?"

Mason said, "I'll put it this way. Certain circumstances have caused me to take an interest in a Helen Reedley who is living at the Siglet Manor Apartments on Eighth Street. I'm wondering whether she is your wife?"

"Why?"

"I'm trying to find out something about her background."

"*What* about her background?"

"Oh, who her friends are, for instance."

"Found out anything?"

"Not yet."

"But you will?"

"I may."

"I might be interested in that."

"Then she *is* your wife?"

"Yes."

"You're separated?"

"Obviously."

"How long have you been separated?"

"Six months."

"You haven't filed suit for divorce?"

"No."

"She hasn't?"

"No."

"Do you intend to?"

"That's none of your business."

"Does she intend to?"

"Ask her."

"Any chance of a reconciliation?"

"That also is none of your business."

"You're not being very coöperative."

"Because I don't propose to show my hand without finding out what kind of game you want to play. What's the object of this visit? What are you after?"

"You've been in communication with her recently?"

"No."

"May I ask when was the last time you talked with her personally?"

"It was about three months ago. I'm telling you certain things that you can find out from other sources, Mason, but I certainly don't intend to let you pump me for information, get up and say 'Thank you,' and walk out."

"Of course," Mason said, "you don't have to tell me anything you don't want to."

"An obvious fact," Reedley said dryly. "What's the occasion of your interest in my wife?"

"Not so much in your wife as in her apartment."

"What about her apartment?"

"A man was murdered there this afternoon."

"Who?"

"A man by the name of Robert Hines."

"You defend people who are accused of murder?"

"Sometimes."

"I take it you're defending someone in this case?"

"No one has been accused, so far as I know."

"Someone who might be accused, then?"

Mason smiled. "Any person might be accused of murder. Records show that many innocent persons have been so accused."

"You're swapping words with me."

"You've been swapping words with me," Mason said. "When you get the best of the trade you see to think that's perfectly fair. When you break even, you crab about it."

Reedley frowned.

"The murder," Mason went on, "doesn't seem to be a surprise to you."

"It's not always easy to tell when I'm surprised and when I'm not."

"I said it didn't *seem* to be a surprise to you."

"Perhaps not."

"Frankly, I wanted some information about your wife."

"Why?"

"I think you can give it to me better than she can."

"What sort of information?"

"You've had detectives shadowing her for the last few days. What have they found out?"

Reedley sat perfectly motionless, his eyes fixed steadily on Mason's face. "Is that a bluff?"

"What do you think?"

"I don't know—that's why I'm asking."

"Asking me if I'm bluffing on the theory that if I am I'll be frank and tell you?" Mason asked.

Again Reedley frowned. "I think you've asked a question I'm not going to answer."

"What I am particularly interested in finding out," Mason said, "is what your wife was doing this afternoon."

"What made you think I'd hired detectives to watch her?"

"Haven't you?"

"I would certainly say that was none of your damn business."

"There are other ways of finding out."

"What?"

"I might tip off some of my friends on the Homicide Squad, or in the D.A.'s office, that if they'd subpoena the head of the Interstate Investigators they could get some interesting information."

Orville Reedley thought that over. Then he asked abruptly, "What good would that do *you*?"

"Put me in solid with the police, and then they'd let me know if they found out you'd put men on the job of shadowing your wife."

"How did you get your lead?"

"I can't tell you that."

"You can't tell me the things I want to know, but you want *me* to tell you the things *you* want to know."

"Exactly."

"That strikes me as being unfair."

"Perhaps it is. You don't have to tell me these things. I *can* go about finding out the hard way."

"Meaning through the police?"

"That's one way."

"Wait a minute," Reedley said, "let me think this over. Don't talk to me for a minute."

He heaved himself out of the chair, paced nervously back and forth across the rug for a few moments, then went over to stand at a window. He adjusted the Venetian blinds so that he could see out, stood moodily staring out of the window for a few seconds, then walked back to the other side of the room, lit a cigarette, took two or three puffs at it, and threw it away.

The telephone rang. "Excuse me a moment," Reedley said. He strode to the telephone and jerked the receiver off the hook. "Well—what is it?"

He was silent for a moment. The words that came over the receiver were faintly audible in the apartment as a steady metallic rattle. When they stopped, he said hesitantly, "I don't know . . ."

Again here was sound from the receiver, followed by a one-word reply from Reedley: "Information."

Another interval of sound, and Reedley said, "Yes . . . That's right . . . Not entirely . . . Getting close to it, I think. Okay, thanks. Keep an eye on things. Okay, good-by."

He hung up and walked back to stand by the table, frowning down at Mason. Then abruptly he turned to Paul Drake. "What are *you* here for?"

"I just came along."

"You're a detective?"

"Yes."

"You're hiring Mason?"

"Other way around—Mr. Mason hires me."

"For what?"

"For the thing a person usually wants out of a detective agency: information."

"You gave him the lead to me?"

"Ask him."

"How did you get it?"

"Ask him."

Mason broke in. "What's the use?" he demanded. "We'll never get anywhere beating around the bush. I learned that detectives had been employed to shadow Helen Reedley. I got Paul Drake to put his men to work shadowing the detectives. The trail led to the Interstate Investigators, and through them to you. They telephoned you when the police discovered the murder of Hines, and you rushed over there and were given information right up to the minute. Then you drove back here."

"Don't you know it's a crime to tap a telephone wire?"

Mason looked him full in the eyes. "No," he said; "is it?"

For a moment there was the suggestion of a twinkle in Reedley's eyes. Then he said, "All right. You've put some cards on the table. I'll match them. I heard that my wife was interested in someone else. I wanted to find out. I put shadows on her. They've been on her for two or three days. This man Hines apparently has been in and out. He's taken her and her chaperone out to dinner, but my wife has never seen him alone. I couldn't figure the deal. However, one of the detectives picked up some information from the police which interests me. When they made a search of the body, they found that Hines had a key to my wife's apartment. It's important to the police and it's important to me to find out how long he'd had it, and how he got it—and why."

"What do *you* think?"

"Use your imagination."

"It sometime leads me astray."

"My wife didn't want to give me a divorce. She's not the type that would retire from circulation and live the life of a recluse. She's had six months. She spent a lot of money having me shadowed. I decided I'd return the compliment."

"She's having you shadowed now?"

"Not now. Up to a couple of months ago she made my life miserable. There was some private detective on my trail every time I turned around. She quit because she couldn't get anything."

"When did you hire these detectives?"

"Two or three days ago."

Mason said, "I think we could swap information to some advantage if you'd be more specific."

"I never make a trade without looking over what I'm going to get."

"The woman your men were shadowing wasn't your wife," Mason told him.

"Don't be silly."

"I'm not."

"What do you mean?"

"I'll put it this way. When you decided to have your wife shadowed, you got in touch with a detective agency. You told them that you wanted to arrange for a twenty-four-hour shadow job, on a woman who was around twenty-three or twenty-four, a brunette, height five feet four and a half inches, weight one hundred and eleven pounds, waist measurement twenty-four inches, bust measurement thirty-two. She lived at Apartment 326 in the Siglet Manor on Eighth Street. You wanted them to keep an eye on the apartment, and pick her up and shadow her every time she went out. You also wanted to know what visitors came to the apartment house and went to see her."

"All right," Reedley said. "So what?"

Mason took a wallet from his pocket, extracted the folded copy of the ad, handed it to Reedley. "That," he said, "is the answer."

Reedley read it through twice before he got its significance. "Well, I'll be double damned!" he said slowly.

"You see what that means," Mason went on. "There was a tip-off. Someone knew in advance that you were going to hire a shadow to trail your wife. Your wife didn't want to be shadowed, so she sidestepped and ran in a ringer. Your detectives put an eye on the apartment you designated. A woman was living there who answered in every way the description that you had given; a woman who could very well have been the person pictured in the snapshot you gave the detective agency."

"I didn't give them any photographs."

"That made it a lot easier," Mason said. "The point I'm making is that here was a tip-off. Someone knew you were going to employ the detective agency two or three days before you actually got the men on the job. Now I want to know where that leak came from."

"*You* want to know," Reedley said angrily. "How the hell do you think *I* feel about it?"

"I thought you'd feel the same way," Mason said. "We might pool our information."

"What information do you have?"

"I've put some of my cards on the table. After you've followed suit, we'll try another lead."

"Look here, Mason," Reedley demanded abruptly. "Don't detective agencies sometimes sell you out? Isn't there a double cross?"

"Sometimes?"

"What do you know about the Interstate Investigators?"

"What do *you* know about them?"

"They were recommended to me by a friend."

"When did you go to them?"

"What do you mean?"

"How soon did you have them put men on the job after you approached them?"

"Almost immediately."

"Then it couldn't have been a leak through the Interstate Investigators. There must have been time for this ad to be inserted, and time for the women to get installed in the apartment; and that must all have been done *before* the Interstate men got on the job. Therefore, there must have been a tip-off two or three days before you went to the detective agency. Who was the friend who recommended that agency?"

"Does that make any difference? I didn't tell him what I intended to do."

"Perhaps you didn't need to. Perhaps you were just asking about some detective agency?"

"I asked him what he knew about the Interstate outfit."

"All right, who was he?"

"I don't think I care to tell you that."

Mason shrugged his shoulders.

There was silence for several seconds. Then Mason turned to Drake and nodded. "I guess that's about all, Paul." And Mason got up.

"Don't go yet," Reedley said. "Sit down."

Mason said, "Hines had a key to your wife's apartment. Have you met Hines?"

"No."

"I've met your wife. She seems to be rather high-voltage."

"High-voltage is right."

"Hines was not exactly a weak sister, but he was sort of nondescript. I can't imagine his appealing to your wife."

"It takes all sorts of people to make a world. You can never tell who is going to appeal to whom."

"That's right. Just the same, Hines impressed me as being rather weak."

"Mason, let's be frank. I don't give a damn if the man was the anemic ruin of a misspent past. If he had a key to Helen's apartment, that's all I want."

"If he'd lived, you'd have named him in a divorce action?"

"I can still use that key business to soften up my wife's demands."

"It might be a two-edged sword," Mason warned him.

"What do you mean by that?"

"Hines was murdered."

"Meaning that . . . Oh, I see."

There were several seconds of silence. Then Reedley said, "Don't be foolish, Mason. I didn't even know the man. I don't like your insinuation."

"I'm not being foolish, and I'm not making any insinuations."

"You're coming damn close to it."

"Not at all. It makes no difference to me. I was merely interested in what course you'd pursue under certain circumstances. Therefore I was pointing out all the facts."

"Well," Reedley admitted, "you pointed out a fact that hadn't occurred to me."

"And that may be important," Mason added.

"It may be damned important," Reedley grudgingly conceded. "Have you any suggestions?"

"About what?"

"About the way to handle that business of the key?"

Mason shook his head. "Ask your lawyer."

"I haven't a lawyer."

"Then I suggest you get one. How about the reports you received from the Interstate people?"

"What about them?"

"You have them here?"

"Yes. That is, the ones sent out yesterday. They mail them out twice a day."

"I'd like to look at them."

"Why?"

"You might say it was merely as a matter of curiosity."

"Just whom do you represent?"

"It might be the brunette who got the job."

"Posing as my wife?"

"I wouldn't say that. She was simply given a job."

"You say you've met my wife?"

"Yes."

"Where?"

"At my office."

"When?"

"Within the last forty-eight hours."

"How much 'within'?"

Mason smiled and shook his head.

"What did she want?"

"It wasn't what *she* wanted—it was what *I* wanted."

"Well, what did you want?"

"I don't think I'm entirely in a position to tell you that."

"Then I'm not in a position to show you the reports of the agents from the Interstate."

"Well, I guess that covers the situation," Mason said with a smile as he got to his feet. "You know where my office is in case you want to give me any information."

"What would I get if I did give it to you?"

"That depends."

"On what?"

"On the information that *you* had, and on the information that *I* had, at the time."

"Okay, I'll think it over."

"Good night," Mason said.

Reedley escorted them to the door, his manner that of a poker player who has sized up a bet and doesn't know whether to quit, raise, or call, but wants a little time to think it over.

7

Back in Drake's car, the detective said, "Gosh, Perry, you certainly did a job on that."

"We didn't get very far," Mason said, a little ruefully.

"Didn't get very far?" Drake echoed. "You got all the information there was. He confirmed the situation you'd suspected about the reason for hiring the brunette actress and all that."

"There's some more to that that I'd like to find out about. Did you notice his apartment, Paul?"

"What about it?"

"He'd evidently furnished it himself."

"Sure. You don't get that type of furniture in furnished apartments, even the swanky ones."

"The whole effect was very—very *harmonious*, wasn't it, Paul?"

"It's a darn swell place, Perry."

"No," Mason contradicted. "The word for it isn't 'swell'—it is 'harmonious." Nice Venetian blinds, beautiful draperies and upholstery, good pictures effectively hung, handsome Oriental rugs, and a lot of excellent furniture—and all in a color scheme that is exactly right."

"What are you getting at?" Drake asked. "What's the apartment got to do with the thing *we're* talking about? It's a swanky apartment, probably sets him back five or six hundred a month unfurnished. So what?"

"You saw what Reedley is like—a man filled with turmoil and restlessness. It's driving him from one thing to another as he goes through life. There's an inner conflict, a desire for power, a certain ruthlessness. He's like a volcano rumbling with molten lava—you can't tell just when he's going to erupt."

"Okay, I'll agree with you on that."

"What I'm getting at," Mason said, "is this: a man with *that* temperament never furnished an apartment in the way *that* one's furnished."

"Oh-oh!" Drake exclaimed.

"You see it now, don't you? There's a woman's touch there. Another thing—did you notice that telephone conversation of his?"

"What about it?"

"He was rather enigmatical."

"It was from the Interstate," Drake said. "They were relaying on some information to him and he was sitting tight because he didn't want to discuss it while we were there."

"What makes you think it was the Interstate?"

"He used the word 'information,' didn't he?"

"Exactly," Mason said. "Now think back a minute. Before the telephone rang, what was he doing?"

"He sat there and talked with us."

"No, he didn't. He got up and walked over to the window. He took a few steps up and down, walking restlessly around, and then he went over to the window. And do you remember what he did *then?*"

"Came back and— No, before he came back he turned the Venetian blind so that he could see out."

"Or so that someone else could see in."

"Well . . . yes," Drake admitted.

"That someone else could have looked into the apartment, could have seen us there, could have telephoned, could have said, 'You have a couple of men up there. What do they want?' And *he* could have said, 'Information.'"

Drake gave a low whistle.

"Of course," Mason said, "I'm just sticking my neck out. But it's a logical deduction. Here we have Reedley, apparently a man of considerable means, with a restless, driving temperament that makes him turn from one thing to another and would naturally make him go from one woman to another. As he gets older, his changes will be made less frequently; but that type of man never celebrates a golden wedding anniversary."

"And you think there's someone there in the apartment house who—"

"Sure. The man's nobody's fool, Paul. His wife has been on his trail with private detectives. She's had him shadowed for months. He knows it. She's kept tabs on his visitors—those she knows about. But suppose he's friendly with a woman in an adjoining apartment? Or suppose he *puts* the woman with whom he's friendly in an adjoining apartment?"

"Gosh, Perry, it's logical all right. It's getting a lot of answers from just one or two clues—sure. But when you stop to think of it, it's the only solution that fits the facts."

"I'm not getting it as a solution," Mason said. "I'm getting it as a clue on which we can work. See if you can't find out who has the adjoining apartment, how long it's been occupied. Get a floor plan of the building. It may not be the adjoining apartment; it may be one of those across the court. But the person must be someone who can see it through that window when Reedley fixes the Venetian blinds right."

"I'll get busy on it, Perry. Anything else?"

"Keep men on Reedley. I don't suppose it will do very much good, but I'd like to know a little more about him."

"Just who is the client in this case, Perry?"

Mason grinned. "Darned if I know. I guess it's Eva Martell. I'd like to get just a little more information in order to protect her in case it becomes necessary. But I think the real truth is that in part I'm my own client. I have some healthy curiosity about what's happening. It's a mystery, and mysteries interest me. I'd like to find out just a little more about Reedley—particularly about how his apartment came to be furnished with such excellent taste."

"Okay, I'll get to work on it. We're going back to your office?"

"That's right. Della's waiting."

Drake turned in at the parking lot next to the office building, and he and Mason went up.

"Coming down to my place?" Mason asked.

"Not unless you want me, Perry. I've got quite a bit of stuff to check up on."

"Okay. Go ahead."

"You'll let me know in case there's anything you want?"

"That's right."

"Any other instructions?"

"Just keep working on the thing. Find out as much about the murder as you can. Get some men investigating that apartment house setup. Keep a shadow on Reedley."

"How about the operatives from the Interstate Investigators?"

"Forget them. You can take your men off them and put them on Reedley."

"Okay, Perry. How do you want your reports?"

"Usual way. If anything's really important, get in touch with me no matter where I am."

"Okay."

Walking on down the corridor, Mason latchkeyed the door to his private office. Della Street looked up, then held up her finger to her lips as a sign for silence.

Mason raised his eyebrows. She gestured with her thumb toward the outer office.

Mason walked quietly over, sat down close to her, and asked in a half-whisper, "What is it?"

"Eva Martell and Adelle Winters are out there."

"Anything new?"

"I don't know. They only arrived about five minutes ago, and all I told them was that I didn't know whether you'd be in any more this evening or not. Thought I'd park them and find out whether you wanted to see them."

"Let's see them," Mason said.

"Now?"

"Uh-huh. Bring them in. Tell them I just came back."

Della Street went out and a moment later returned with Eva Martell and Adelle Winters.

"Well," Mason said, "you seem to have run into quite a bit of excitement."

"I'll say we did," Eva said.

"Sit down and tell me about it."

"Well, there isn't much to tell. We went back to the apartment and let ourselves in with the key Mr. Hines had given us and started making ourselves at home. I had taken off my hat and coat and was just going into the bathroom when I saw him."

"Where was he?"

"In a big chair in the bedroom. All slumped down. And that bullet hole in his forehead, and the blood down the side of his face and over the shoulder of his shirt—it was terrible!"

"What did you do?" Mason asked.

"Screamed her head off," Adelle Winters said, interposing her competent personality as a barrier between Mason and further questioning of the girl. "I clapped my hand over her mouth and told her to be her age. I went over and took a look at him, saw he was dead, and told her to telephone you for instructions."

"He was shot in the forehead?" Mason asked.

"Yes—right between the eyes."

"Did you notice any powder burns?"

"I didn't look for them, but I didn't see any."

"I understand he was shot with a .32 revolver."

Mrs. Winters shrugged her shoulders.

"You had a .32 revolver, I believe, Mrs. Winters. You'd better—"

"Who? Me?"

"You did have one, didn't you?"

She threw back her head and laughed. "Good heavens, no!"

"Why, I thought you said that . . ."

"Oh, that's just one of my little ways of running a bluff,

78

Mr. Mason. I've never yet seen the man that I had to be afraid of, but it doesn't do any harm to let them think they're dealing with a hellcat, so I always *tell* 'em that I'm carrying a gun. It's a good bluff."

Mason frowned. "You told me you carried a gun and had no permit to do so. I told you to get rid of the gun or else get a permit to carry it."

Her eyes twinkled at him. "And you remember I wasn't a darn bit worried about not having a permit for it. That's because I didn't really have any gun—so naturally I wasn't worried at all."

Eva interrupted. "But *I* always thought you carried a gun. You told me you did, several times, Aunt Adelle."

Mrs. Winters chuckled delightedly. "Well, it made you feel safer because I told you that, didn't it? I'll run a bluff, but when something like this comes up, there's no percentage in sticking your neck out."

Mason was watching her with a puzzled frown on his forehead. "Now, let's be frank about this," he said. "If you *did* have a gun, the police are pretty likely to find out you had it. Then if you deny it . . ."

"Good heavens, Mr. Mason, what a fuss you make over what was just a plain bluff! I never carried a gun in my life."

"That's your final answer?"

"Of course it is. It's the truth."

"How long had Hines been dead when you found him?"

"Well, I couldn't say. The body was still warm, but . . . well, sort of lukewarm. It's pretty hard to tell about the temperature of a body without putting your hand inside the clothes somewhere. I just touched his wrist. His coat was hung on the chair."

"Felt for his pulse?"

"That's right."

"Touch anything else?"

"No."

"You didn't go through the clothes at all?"

"Good heavens, why should I go through his clothes?"

"Were you with her all the time?" Mason asked, turning to Eva Martell.

"What's the idea of asking questions like that?" Adelle Winters exclaimed irritably. "That's the same sort of stuff the police have been asking."

"I was just trying to find out."

"Yes, I was with her all the time," Eva Martell said.

"How about when you were telephoning to me?"

"Well, that was just a second or two."

"And you've been together all day?"

"That's right."

"Every minute of the time?"

"Every single solitary minute."

"Well, that's going to help."

"That's the way the police looked at it," Adelle Winters said.

"Did the officers ask you how you happened to be living in that apartment?"

"Of course they did."

"What did you tell them?"

"Told them the complete truth."

"You told them all about Hines and how he had hired you?"

"Yes."

"To impersonate Helen Reedley?"

"We weren't impersonating anyone," Adelle Winters said. "We took a job and he asked us to take a certain name for the job."

"But you told them about me?"

"That's right."

"About how I got in touch with Helen Reedley?"

"Well, no," Adelle Winters said. "We didn't tell them *too* much."

"What did you tell them?"

"We told them that we had this job and that you told us you didn't want us to go ahead with it until you were positive it was all right, so that we wouldn't be guilty of any crime. So we said you investigated and reported that it was all right; so then we went shopping, had dinner, and returned to the apartment. And when we returned, we found the body."

"You didn't tell them about being shadowed?"

"No."

"And did you tell them anything else?"

"What else is there to tell? We just were hired and went to work, and that's all there was to it. We didn't know what the job was, but we certainly weren't impersonating anyone. And we didn't defraud anyone."

"Did the police seem to think there was some scheme back of it?"

"No, to tell you the truth, Mr. Mason, the police didn't seem so interested in that part. They seemed to know Hines—he had a police record for racetrack gambling. They didn't even ask us for the phone number where we'd been calling him, and so we didn't give it to them. I *think* they'd talked with some of the men who had been shadowing us. I don't know for certain, but I think so. I saw one of them waiting there in the apartment house and thought he was waiting to be questioned."

Mason said, "I guess they probably already had a statement from him. As a matter of fact, those were two detectives who had been hired to keep an eye on you. They'd been following you everywhere you went ever since you'd been on the job."

"Well now, isn't *that* something!" Adelle Winters exclaimed. "Great goings-on when a couple of respectable women are trying to make an honest living and detectives start traipsing around after them."

"Did the police tell you to keep in touch with them?"

"No. I told them I'd be at my apartment, and Eva Martell told them she'd be back with Cora Felton. The police took the addresses and said they'd get in touch with us if there was anything else they wanted. But they seem to think it was a gambling murder."

"Oh," said Mason. "Well, I guess that's about all, then."

Adelle Winters got to her feet and nodded to Eva Martell. "We thought we'd drop in and tell you, Mr. Mason—you've been so nice to us."

"I'm glad you did."

"I guess . . . Well, Cora Felton hired you to see that everything was all right with us, and I guess now . . . Well, I guess there's nothing more to do. We don't want to run up too much of a bill, you know."

Mason laughed. "You won't."

"But we don't want *you* to be loser either, Mr. Mason. There isn't anything more to do now, is there?"

"It's hard to say just what the situation is."

"Well, I think it would be better if you just—you know—let the whole thing drop and tell us how much we owe you, and that'll be that. We'll pay up. And how about this extra money we got from Hines? The amount that was over what we had coming to us?"

"Did you tell the police about that?"

"Well, no, I didn't. I told them he'd paid us up to date, and they didn't ask me how much, so I didn't tell them."

"Well, that's right. You are paid up to date. In any event, the police won't have anything to do with that phase of it. That will be up to the executor of Hines's estate."

"You mean that we don't need to tell anyone just how much we received?"

"Not until the executor asks you. And then you can tell him that what you got was as a payment for services performed and in the nature of a guarantee that the contract would be carried out—so that if anything interfered you'd be assured of your money."

"I see. Thank you, Mr. Mason. Good night."

"Good night," Mason said.

Eva Martell, turning impulsively, gave Mason her hand and a flash of gratitude from dark eyes. "Thank you," she said in a low voice. "You've been *so* kind. Will we see you again?"

"Perhaps."

"I thought perhaps you'd drop in and have a drink with us, and there might be some questions you'd want to ask some time in the future."

"There won't be a thing," Adelle Winters said positively. "The case is all closed as far as Mr. Mason is concerned. Come on, Eva."

A few minutes after they had left, Mason't private phone rang. Since only Della Street and Paul Drake knew that number, Mason scooped up the receiver and said, "Yes, hello, Paul. What is it?"

"Something red-hot, Perry. And I mean it *is* red-hot."

"Shoot."

"Well, the police got those Interstate men on the carpet and gave them a pretty thorough grilling. They made the boys kick through with everything they had."

"Naturally the police would do that," Mason said. "What happened?"

"Well, the boys turned in their notes, giving a complete picture of what had been done with shadowing operations on the two women, telling exactly where they went, the license numbers of the cabs they took—all that kind of thing."

"What's wrong with that?" Mason asked.

"Well, it seems that at two-twenty this afternoon, very shortly after the two women got to that hotel where they went and waited, Adelle Winters went exploring. In a passageway she found a lot of garbage cans from the kitchen waiting to be picked up by the garbage man. She lifted the cover of one of the garbage cans and looked in. The man who was shadowing her made a note of what she had done, but didn't pay much attention to it."

"Okay, Paul, go ahead. What happened?"

"Well," Drake said, "the police did pay some attention to it, as a matter of routine check-up; they thought she might have been ditching something. They rushed a couple of the boys down to the hotel. By that time the cans were pretty well filled with garbage, but the Interstate man was able to point out the one that Mrs. Winters had looked into. So the police spread out a canvas and dumped out the contents—and what do you think they found?"

"Well—what?"

"A .32-caliber revolver with one chamber fired," Drake said.

Mason whistled.

"And," Drake went on, "the bullets were of a certain old-fashioned obsolete type. Exactly the same as the bullet the autopsy surgeon has taken from the head of Robert Hines. Of course, they haven't made tests in the Ballistics Department yet to make *certain* that the bullet was fired from that particular gun. But nine hundred and ninety-nine chances out of a thousand it was. That mean anything to you, Perry?"

"It means a hell of a lot to me. Della!" Mason shouted, turning from the phone, "sprint down the corridor. Try and get those women before they get to the elevator and bring them back. Wait a minute—Paul, you're closer to the elevator—dash out and stop them. They've just left the office."

"Right away," Drake said, and slammed up the receiver.

Ten minutes later Drake was back in Mason's office. "Missed them at the elevator, Perry. There's only one cage running at this hour of night. By the time I managed to get it up to this floor they'd had time enough to make a getaway. I got out of the car and took a look around the block, but couldn't see anyone answering the description of the pair you wanted. According to the elevator man, they must have had a head start of a minute and a half or two minutes, which is a lot of time in a situation of this sort."

"Well, I know where they live," Mason said, "and I can get them. But I've got to see them before the police do."

Drake grinned. "And the police would like to see them before you do. Is she your client, Perry—the Winters woman?"

"I don't think she is. I was retained to look out for Eva."

"Of course," Drake pointed out, "the girl could have a clean nose. The Winters woman could have been a lone wolf. By the way, Perry, Eva Martell told the police Hines'd had a wallet pretty well stacked with dough. It wasn't there when the police searched."

"He had a wallet all right. You say there was no money on the body?"

"Less than ten bucks."

"Did Eva say she was with Adelle Winters all the time?"

"Every minute. That's why the police let 'em go. Their story seemed okay, and each of 'em gave an alibi for the other."

Mason said, "But Eva Martell wasn't with her *all* the time—I know that much. She was talking with me on the telephone for a while, and . . . Gosh, Paul, I'd like to get hold of her and get her to change her statement and tell the truth. I suppose the old gal has a lot of influence over her—though even at that, you can't see Eva standing by while her friend pumped the .32 bullet between Hines's eyebrows. It must has been that when they left the apartment Mrs. Winters stayed on for a few minutes and then joined Eva Martell on the sidewalk; or perhaps after they had left the apartment Mrs. Winters thought of something she had forgotten and went back to get it. Then, later on, after they'd 'found' the corpse, Mrs. Winters could have told Eva it would simplify matters for her if Eva would swear they'd been together all the time. And Eva, thinking that of course there was no possible chance her friend had committed a murder, gave the police that story."

"Well," Drake said, "I'm sure sorry I couldn't catch up with them. I cruised around the block. They must have had a cab."

"It's all right," Mason said. "I'd like to have caught up with them, but I think I can reach them. What was that number Cora Felton left us, Della? That's where Eva will be going. Put through a call and . . . I'll tell you what you do: get Cora Felton on the line."

Della Street nodded, consulted the file cards that listed clients' telephone numbers, and put through the call.

The waited an anxious ten seconds. Then Della shook her head. "No answer."

Mason said, "Do we have the number of Adelle Winter's place?"

"I think so. Yes."

"There's not one chance in a hundred that the police won't be on the job there. They'll nail her the minute she shows up. But see what you can do, Della."

Della Street tried that number without success.

"All right. Try Cora Felton again."

Again there was no answer.

"I guess there's only one thing to do, Paul," said Mason. "You and I will go down and wait at Cora Felton's apartment. Della will stay here."

"Della, in case Eva Martell telephones, which she may do, get her out of circulation and notify me. In the meantime, I'll have my car and be waiting at the girls' apartment. If I can get her before the police do, I'll see what can be done. Come on. Paul."

8

With Paul Drake sitting in silence beside him, Mason drove out to Cora Felton's apartment house. He cruised slowly around the block, cautiously sizing up the situation. There were two cars parked within half a block of each other; and two men occupied each one of the cars. One car was up the street from the apartment house entrance; the other was down the street. Both cars were so parked, however, that the men inside could watch the entrance. They were husky, well-fed, broad-shouldered. Mason, sizing them up, dared not circle the block more than once.

"What do you make of it, Paul?" he asked.

"Nothing to it," Drake said. "The cops have the place sewed up."

"Of course they don't know Cora Felton."

"Don't be too sure. They've probably talked with the manager of the apartment house. They knew all about where your client was living, and with whom she's living. They've got a description of Cora Felton and they'll nail her just on general principles. They don't want anyone left in the apartment and answering the telephone."

"I suppose so," Mason said. "Hang it, I hate to give up—it seems like throwing the kid to the wolves. Say, Paul, there's a chance that those two mightn't squander money on a taxicab. Where's the nearest streetcar line? You know the city."

"Three blocks down the street."

"Which way?"

"Straight ahead," Drake said.

Mason drove rapidly until he reached a line of car tracks,

then swung in to the curb, parked the car, shut off the motor, and switched off the headlights. "This is the only chance we have, Paul. Any sign of cops?"

"None that I see. They've set their trap back at the apartment."

Mason was drawing on a cigarette. "At this hour of the night," he said thoughtfully, "the streetcars run only every fifteen or twenty minutes. If those two caught a streetcar in front of our office building, they should be getting here about now."

"Say, wait a minute—what'll you do if they do show up?"

"Talk with them," Mason said laconically.

"And then turn them over to the police, of course. *After* you've heard their story?"

"I can't tell."

"Now wait a minute," Drake said. "You know what the police found out about Adelle Winters."

"Well?"

"You know what that means. She killed him. It may have been in self-defense, or it may not. But she did kill him, and she tried to lie out of it. And Eva Martell is mixed in it right along with Adelle."

"Well?"

"You keep them out of circulation, knowing the police are looking for them on a murder rap, and that makes you an accessory. I don't think I want to get mixed up in that sort of deal. . . ."

"Make up your mind, Paul. Here comes a streetcar."

"My mind's made up. If you're going to keep them from the police, I'm going to bail out."

The streetcar was plainly visible now. "You can probably get a taxi without much trouble," Mason said.

"It doesn't make any difference how much trouble it is, I'm taking a powder. That car's stopping—and there are two women getting ready to get out. Good night, Perry."

" 'Night, Paul," Mason said, adding in an undertone,

"Don't let the police catch you hanging around the neighborhood."

Drake paused. "Perry, have a heart! Don't stick you neck out in this thing. Talk with them, and then notify the police. The police will get them anyway."

"I'll probably do that."

"Promise?"

"No."

"Why?"

"I may change my mind after I hear what they tell me. Here they are, Paul."

"On my way," Drake said. "And I think I'll stay on this streetcar until I get clean out of the neighborhood!"

He gave a shrill whistle and sprinted for the car. Mason switched on his headlights, turned his car around and, when the two were abreast of him, opened the door. "Hello, Eva," he said. "Is that Mrs. Winters with you?"

It was Cora Felton who answered. "Well, I like *that!*"

Mason laughed. "In this light, all I could make out was just two figures. How about a lift?"

"The apartment's only two or three blocks away, but that'll be fine."

"I want to talk with you a minute before you go to the apartment. You have company there."

"Who?" Eva Martell asked.

"The police."

"But you've already talked with them. At least I have."

"They want to talk some more."

"Good heavens, Mr. Mason, I've told them absolutely everything I know."

"Where's Mrs. Winters?"

"She went on to her apartment."

"On that streetcar?"

"No, I transferred. The car we took in front of your office building took Aunt Adelle directly home."

"Then she's probably home ahead of you."

"I'll say she is. I had to wait ten minutes for a car at the transfer point."

"Where were you?" Mason asked Cora Felton.

"I happened to be on the same car—just a coincidence. I'd been to a movie. I certainly was surprised when Eva got aboard and told me what had happened."

"I'll feel better," Mason said, "if I get you both out of the neighborhood while we talk. Let's drive out a little way and park the car."

"Why do we have to talk? What's it all about?" Eva asked. "I thought we'd finished everything."

Mason was driving the car slowly along the road and keeping a watch in the rear view mirror. "You told the police that you had been with Adelle Winters all day?" he asked her.

"Yes."

"Why did you tell them that?"

"Because it's the truth."

"Did you sign a statement to that effect?"

"Yes."

"Swear to it?"

"Yes. It was an affidavit."

"I'm not the police. Don't lie to me. I'm your lawyer— tell me the truth. Now were you with her *all* day?"

"Yes."

"Every minute of the time?"

"Well . . . I . . . practically."

"Never mind that 'pratically' stuff. Tell me the truth."

"Well, there were a few minutes here and there around the hotel—for instance when she went to the rest room. . . ."

"But how about before you went to the hotel?—while you were still at the apartment?"

"Well . . . but, Mr. Mason, what difference does it make?"

Mason was impatient. "Heaven knows why I waste time

on you. Do I have to drag the truth out of you with a block and tackle? Go ahead and tell me what happened."

With a nervous laugh she obeyed. "Well, of course, it doesn't mean a darned thing, but after we left the apartment and got down to the lobby, we stopped to put through some phone calls from the booth there. After we'd been there a few minutes, Aunt Adelle suddenly remembered that she'd left something of hers in the apartment, and she wanted to go up and get it."

"What was it?"

"Well, she *told* me—after we got to the hotel—that it was a .32 revolver. She said she'd had it in a sideboard drawer, had taken it out, then had inadvertently left it on the sideboard, intending to put it in her handbag, and . . . well, she'd just forgotten it. She didn't want to leave it there. So I waited in the apartment-house lobby, reading, and she took the key and ran back up to the apartment. Of course, now that she says she never owned a gun . . . well, I hardly know what to think."

"How did it happen you didn't mention this to the police?"

"Isn't that obvious, Mr. Mason? When we got back to the apartment later and found Hines with a bullet hole in his forehead, Aunt Adelle said the only thing to do was to get in touch with you. And you told us to notify the police. Then Aunt Adelle suggested that there'd be no sense in complicating the situation by mentioning that she'd left something up in the apartment."

"Did she tell you it was a gun she had left there?"

"Not then. She had told me that back at the hotel."

"What time was it when she went upstairs for the gun?"

"Around two o'clock. It was just before we left the apartment house. Perhaps ten minutes after two—I'd looked at my watch as we left the elevator, and it was five to two then. We were in the lobby some ten or fifteen minutes, what with one thing and another. It was probably a minute or so past two when she started back to the apartment upstairs."

Mason said, "Now this is terribly important. Where were *you?*"

"You mean while Aunt Adelle went back upstairs?"

"Yes."

"In the lobby."

"You're sure?"

"Yes."

"Not outside, where any person who had been shadowing you could have seen you?"

"No. I waited inside the lobby reading a racing form sheet."

"How long was she gone?"

"Oh, just a few minutes."

"Can you make a better estimate than that?"

"Well, perhaps five or six minutes."

"But it couldn't have taken so long as that for her just to go up to the apartment and back, could it?"

"It must have—there was no other place for her to go. Mr. Mason, what is the reason for all these questions?"

"Adelle Winters had a gun, and that gun killed Robert Hines."

"What?"

"That's right."

"Are you certain?"

"Practically certain. The Ballistics Department hasn't given its report yet, but the police found Mrs. Winter's gun."

"Where?"

"Where she had been seen to put it, in a garbage pail at the Lorenzo Hotel."

"And you mean the bullet had been fired from that gun? Why, Mr. Mason, that's utterly impossible!"

"Although Mrs. Winters had bought some fresh ammunition, she hadn't as yet reloaded the gun. It was loaded with shells of obsolete type, and the bullet was quite distinctive—it was exactly the same type that the police recovered from the skull of Robert Hines."

"Why, that's aboslutely incredible!"

"All right, let's see what Adelle Winters has to say. Let's see what her story is about the gun. Did you believe her when she said she didn't have a gun—that it was all a bluff?"

"No, I didn't. That's the funny thing about Aunt Adelle. You have to take some of the things that she says with a . . . Well, it isn't exactly that she *wants* to deceive you; it's just—well, it's hard to explain. You see, she's been a practical nurse, and she's nursed a lot of persons with incurable diseases. So she got into the way of lying, reasssuring them, telling them they were going to get well. Or, if she was nursing someone who'd had a nervous breakdown, she'd lie to keep her patient from worrying, telling things that would help toward the sick person's recovery. If you could only see Aunt Adelle in that light, you'd understand the whole thing."

"In other words, she's a liar!"

"If you want to put it bluntly, she is. She believes in avoiding trouble by detouring facts."

"And you were sure she was lying about not having a gun?"

"I always felt she had a gun—yes."

"And suppose she's lying about what happened there in the apartment?"

"No, that wouldn't be like Aunt Adelle at all. Can't we go talk with her?"

"I'm afraid the police are waiting at her apartment."

"We might drive there and find out."

"It's a waste of gasoline, but we've got to try it. You show me the way. The main thing, as I see it, is to get you in the clear."

"How do you mean?"

"You told the police you had been with Adelle Winters 'all the time.' Now if her gun killed Robert Hines, you must have been with her when the shot was fired—and that has put you in quite a mess. The police are waiting out at your apartment. You'll be charged as an accessory. I want to get *you* in the clear. Later we'll see what can be done for Aunt Adelle."

"But we'll first make certain that she isn't at her apartment?"

"Exactly," Mason said.

"How?"

"We'll drive out there, then Cora can scout out the situation."

"All right," Eva said. "You drive straight down this street."

Mason and the two girls drove to the place where Adelle Winters had her apartment, an unpretentious three-story thirty-five minutes by streetcar from the center of the city.

A knot of curious spectators milling around told the story even before Cora had slipped out to mingle unobtrusively with them and pick up the news. She was back within five minutes.

"They nabbed her?" Mason asked.

Cora nodded. "They picked her up just as she was entering the apartment. They shot a lot of questions at her and Adelle got confused. They showed her a gun and asked her if it was hers. She admitted it was. That's all anybody knows. They put her in an automobile and drove away."

Mason said, "Okay." He turned to Eva. "I'm going to lead with my chin, Eva. I'm going to put you someplace where the police can't find you tonight, and then make a bargain with the D.A.'s office tomorrow."

Eva Martell asked, "Why can't I tell my story to the police right now?"

Mason shook his head. "I've got to get you a promise of immunity, and I won't be in a good bargaining position unless I have something to bargain with."

9

Harry Gulling, who was considered the wheel-horse of the district attorney's office, was rarely seen in court; only occasionally did his name appear in the public press. But those who were on the inside knew that Hamilton Berger, the district attorney, relied on Gulling to make important decisions. Those who knew the ropes would never think of trying to make a deal with Hamilton Berger until they had first seen Harry Gulling and obtained a clearance through him.

It was nine-forty-five in the morning when Mason was ushered into Gulling's office. Mason shook hands, sat down opposite Gulling—he was a tall, thin man who had a trick of holding people with an unwinking stare from cold blue eyes—and said, "I'm representing Eva Martell. She was living in Helen Reedley's apartment with a woman named Adelle Winters. I believe you're holding the Winters woman on suspicion of murder."

Harry Gulling remained motionless, his glacial blue eyes framing pinpoint pupils as he listened. Now he said nothing, but just waited for Mason to go on.

"I think my client can be of some help to you," Mason said.

"How?"

"Well, perhaps—and mind you I'm only saying *perhaps*—her testimony might be of some assistance."

"What?"

"Suppose that after thinking back over the events of yesterday she remembered that she had *not* been with

Adelle Winters all the time. I assume you're familiar with the case?"

"I've just finished questioning Mrs. Winters," Gulling said, "and here on my desk are the police reports."

"Very well. Then we're in a position to talk turkey. Eva Martell is a young woman who is trying to get by—playing parts here and there, sometimes as an extra, and by serving as a model. She's never had any experience before with this sort of thing. Adelle Winters, who's an old friend of Eva's family, is apparently something of a character. Whether or not she's guilty of murder is a matter for you to determine. But you have the murder weapon, and I understand you have identified it as belonging to Adelle Winters. In view of the statement given you yesterday by Eva Martell, you could hardly expect to get a conviction, because you simply can't show that Adelle Winters had any chance to commit the murder.

"Now I'm frank to admit that my client ought to have searched her recollection a little more thoroughly. Perhaps she was trying to protect Adelle Winters. Perhaps she was confused. But let's say that in the excitement of the day's events she neglected to tell you of a time when Adelle Winters was *not* with her. Then what?"

Gulling kept his eyes on Mason's face. "Where is your client now?"

"She can be produced in a very short time if necessary."

"The police want her."

"She'll be only too glad to render what assistance she can to the police."

"And exactly what do you want?"

"What's the use of beating around the bush?" Mason asked. "I understand Eva Martell signed a statement and swore to it. In case that statement contains an incorrect recital of fact, I want to be sure that nothing is going to be done about it."

"So that's it?"

"That's it."

"And that's the reason you're jockeying for position around here instead of bringing your client in and having her say, 'Look, I made a mistake.'"

"Of course it is," Mason said eagerly. "What the hell did you think? That I was going to lead with my chin?"

"You *have* led with it."

"Bosh!" exclaimed Mason.

"Adelle Winters is guilty of cold-blooded murder. We can prove it. Your client is an accessory after the fact—and probably before the fact."

"Hang it, Gulling, if my client doesn't come out in the open and admit she's mistken, but simply sits tight, what the hell are you going to do about it?"

"You've asked a question," Gulling said. "Now I'll tell you the answer. Adelle Winters had a .32-caliber gun and it was loaded with a very distinctive type of obsolete bullet. That gun was in her possession up until two-twenty yesterday afternoon, when she dropped it into a garbage pail. At approximately two o'clock Robert Hines was killed with a bullet fired from that gun—a bullet exactly matching the shells that were left in the gun, and also matching a bullet that the ballistics experts fired from that gun.

"Eva Martell swears she was with Adelle Winters every minute of the time. That being the case, we're going to convict both of them for murder. And I'll tell you how we're going to do it, Mr. Mason. When police took Adelle Winters into custody last night, the matron went through her clothes and took her personal possessions. And what do you think she found?"

Mason tried to keep a poker face. "I don't see that anything she could have found would make any difference."

"Don't you indeed, Mr. Mason!" Gulling said with cold irony. "Well, perhaps you'll change your mind when I tell you that she found Robert Dover Hines's wallet with his indentification cards, his driving license, and three thousand-odd dollars in currency of large denominations. *There's* your motive for murder. And when your sweet, innocent little actress friend gets on the witness stand and swears that she was with Adelle Winters every minute of the time, she's going to be convicted of first-degree murder. And if she changes her story, she's going to be convicted of perjury. I'm tired of having people give this office the run-around.

"And I'm going to tell you something else, Mr. Mason. Eva Martell is wanted by the police. They hold a felony warrant for her arrest. She is now a fugitive from justice. If you conceal her, you yourself will be an accessory, and you know what that means. I'll give you until noon today to have Eva Martell surrender to the police. In the event she doesn't, we'll take proceedings against you. And I think that represents everything this office has to say on the subject. Good morning, Mr. Mason."

10

Mason sat on one side of the heavy, coarse-meshed screen that ran the length of the visitors' room in the jail. On the other side sat Adelle Winters.

"Mrs. Winters," Mason said, "I'm going to put the cards on the table. I was trying to help Eva Martell, and I thought at the time it was an easy case—now I find out that it isn't."

"Why isn't it?"

"Because of the things *you* have done. Police feel that you and Eva deliberately planned to murder Hines for the purpose of getting his money."

"That's absurd!"

"They can build up a pretty strong case."

"Eva is absolutely innocent. But *I'm* in a mess—I know that."

"You seem to have dragged Eva in with you."

"But I wouldn't have done that for worlds! I love that girl like a daughter. Are you going to be my lawyer, Mr. Mason?"

"I don't think so. I got in here because I told the jailer that I had to talk with you as an attorney to find out whether I'd take your case. That still holds true. But what I want to know is where Eva stands in this."

"Well, I'll tell you what happened, Mr. Mason. When you spoke to me about the danger of carrying that gun, I pretended not to pay any attention. Actually I was very much impressed. I realized that someone might make it appear we had committed a technical crime. And as I understand it, there's a law that if you have a gun in your possession when you're committing a crime, you can't get probation—you have to go to the penitentiary."

"Well, I decided to get rid of the gun. From your office I went back up to the apartment, and the first thing I did there was to take the gun out of my purse and put it in the sideboard drawer. Then—later, when we were planning to get out—I took it out of the drawer and put it on top of the sideboard. But in the excitement of gathering my things together and getting out, I forgot it. Down in the lobby I did some telephoning. I called Hines several times, and got no answer. I called you, and kept hearing the busy signal. Then I suddenly remembered about the gun. So I told Eva to wait—that I had forgotten something and had to go back upstairs."

"What time was this?"

"Oh, perhaps two o'clock, perhaps a little after."

"So what did you do?"

"I went up in the elevator, walked along the corridor, opened the door of the apartment. The gun was there on the sideboard. At the time, I didn't notice anything strange about it; but afterwards I recalled that when I'd left it the muzzle had been pointing toward the wall, though when I picked it up the muzzle was pointing toward me. The door to the bedroom was closed. I didn't open it—fortunately. The murderer must have been in there right then.

"So I picked up the gun, turned toward the door, and then noticed that wallet lying on the floor near the bedroom door. I swear to you, Mr. Mason, I didn't any more than look at it, see that it was Mr. Hines's wallet, and push it down inside my blouse. I intended to give it to him when I saw him, which I thought would be soon.

"I left the apartment and picked up Eva, and we took a cab to the Lorenzo Hotel; it took less than five minutes. At the hotel I went at once to the ladies' room and opened my purse to get my compact. When I did that, I smelled a peculiar powder smell. It came from the gun, of course. So I looked at it, and one shell had been fired. I smelled of the barrel, and it smelled of fresh powder. I wanted to get rid of it, so I took it out to that garbage pail and dumped it in.

"And that's the real, honest-to-goodness truth, Mr. Mason—every word of it!"

"*I* want to believe your story, Mrs. Winters," Mason told her. "*I'm* anxious to believe you're innocent. But the story you have just told doesn't convince me, and I don't see how you can possibly expect a jury to believe it."

"Oh, I can improve on it, Mr. Mason, if I have time," she assured him.

"You mean you're going to change that story?"

"Sure—to make it better."

"Regardless of the facts?"

She snorted. "Facts don't mean a damn thing. Lots of times, the truth isn't very convincing. But I'm pretty good at fixing up stories, Mr. Mason, and I can improve this one considerably. As it is, I've told you the real truth—I wouldn't tell that to anyone else."

"You want me to believe that *after* you first left the apartment, and went down to the lobby, and then came back up in the elevator, both Hines and the murderer walked in without your seeing them; that they walked into the bedroom; that the murderer killed Hines with your gun that he had picked up from the sideboard; that he replaced the gun, took Hines's wallet and threw it on the floor, and then was trapped in the bedroom by your return?"

"That's right."

"That's the way it happened?"

"That's the way it *must* have happened."

Mason looked at her. "That is," he went on, "just to make the thing more convincing, the murderer took that wallet containing something over three thousand dollars and tossed it on the floor, so that you could find it and walk off with it?"

"You don't believe me, do you, Mr. Mason?"

"No."

"That's exactly the way it happened. Cross my heart and hope to die, Mr. Mason, I'm telling you the truth."

"How do you suppose Hines got into the apartment house without your seeing him?"

"I don't know." There was a moment of silence. Then she said, "He *had* to get there, Mr. Mason. If he was killed with my gun, he *had* to be there before I left—no matter who killed him. His body was there in the bedroom."

"It was for a fact," the lawyer conceded. Then he asked abruptly, "How about that number Hines gave you so that you could call him? Did he tell you where the phone was located?"

"No."

"And while you were telephoning, you didn't see him come into the apartment house? Neither you nor Eva saw him enter?"

"No—nobody came in during the few minutes we were there before I started upstairs."

Mason said, "There's one way of putting the facts together so your story isn't quite so implausible. I'll investigate that theory."

"What's that?"

"That Hines lived in another apartment in the same building, and that was the apartment where the telephone was located."

"Yes. That's so. That must be it. That *would* make my story sound better, wouldn't it?"

Mason studied her.

"Now you're sure this story you've told is the truth."

"It's the truth, Mr. Mason," she said, and after a moment added, "but I haven't a damn bit of confidence in it."

11

From a phone booth in the reception room at the jail, Mason called Paul Drake.

"How are you coming?" Paul asked.

"Not so good," Mason admitted, "but I have a lead, Paul."

"What?"

"Have Della give you the telephone number the girls were instructed to call in order to get in touch with Robert Hines. Find out where that phone is located. I'm particularly anxious to find out whether Hines had an apartment there in the Siglet Manor on Eighth Street."

"I think the police have dug up everything there is to know about your friend Hines," Drake said. "He didn't live there—he lived in a downtown residential hotel and had had the same room there for five years. He was single, and rather taciturn; he played the ponies occasionally, and seems to have done a bit of sharp-shooting here and there. He was tighter than the bark on a tree when it came to putting money out."

"Just check on that telephone number anyway, Paul. It's important. Get me the lowdown on it as soon as you can. What have you found out about that apartment where Reedley hangs out? Or rather, about his neighbor?"

"We may have struck pay dirt there, Perry. Her name's Daphne Gridley. She's a commercial artist. She's also done some work as an interior decorator. She's been there five or six years in the apartment house, and apparently it was through her efforts that Reedley got the apartment he's in now."

"What does she look like, Paul?"

"Class."

"How old?"

"Twenty-six or twenty-seven."

"Blonde or brunette?"

"Chestnut-haired."

"Knows her way around?"

"I think so."

"Making money?"

"She inherited a flock of it five or six years ago. She only does the art stuff to keep busy."

"Well, it doesn't do us any particular good, Paul, except that it checks with what we discovered. There's a certain amount of personal satisfaction in that."

"What *you* discovered," Drake corrected. "And you just can't ever tell. It might help if you had something on Reedley, and I think I can find out a little more if I go to work on the Gridley woman. How about it?"

"Use your judgment. I seem to have a bear by the tail and I'm going to need all the help I can get. Chase down that number right away, Paul. I'll call you back inside of twenty to thirty minutes."

"Okay," Drake said, "I suppose the police will have beaten us to it, but there's no harm in giving it the once-over. They can't rule you off for trying, Perry."

"Trying is right. I've got to hit the high spots. However, I have a hunch the police *may* not know about this. Hines was mixed up in some gambling activities, and the police know all about those. But it wouldn't surprise me to learn that they hadn't bothered to chase down that phone number— perhaps they didn't even get it from the women. Well, I'll call you back."

"Okay," Drake said. "But you'd better play them pretty close to your chest, Perry. This is beginning to look a little tough for the Winters woman."

"Are you telling me!" Mason said. "And the worst bit of

evidence you don't even know. Well, I'm not representing *her*—that's one consolation."

Mason hung up, returned to his auto, and drove a dozen blocks to a rooming house run by a woman who had once been a client."

"Hello, Mae," Mason said. "How's our girl friend?"

"Fine, Mr. Mason. She's in 211. I took up some breakfast to her about an hour and a half ago. She doesn't want to be any trouble and didn't want to bother me, but I told her you said she mustn't be seen in public until you had things fixed up."

"Right," Mason said. "Thanks a lot, Mae."

Mae Bagley was a tall blonde woman in the early thirties. Her face could be hard, but as she looked at Perry Mason her eyes softened. "I didn't even put her on the register, Mr. Mason, just in case they did get a tip-off or anything. Two-eleven is supposed to be vacant."

"You shouldn't have done that, Mae."

"You said to bury her, and when you say anything—well, that's all there is to it."

"That's nice of you, but it's taking chances—"

"I'd take 'em for you any day, Mr. Mason."

"Thanks, Mae. You're a good egg. I'll go on up."

Mason climbed the stairs to the second floor and tapped on the door of 211.

Eva Martell opened it so quickly that it seemed she must have been sitting by the door waiting for the lawyer's arrival. She was dressed for the street and her face lit up when she saw who it was.

"Oh, I'm *so* glad to see you! I thought it was the woman coming for the dishes. I wanted to take them down to her, but she said you had . . . But do come in and sit down. Here—take this chair, it's the most comfortable. I'll sit over here by the window."

Mason seated himself, took out his cigarette case, opened it, and offered her a cigarette. She shook her head. "I've been smoking too much, and I'm getting a bit nervous. Just waiting, not knowing what's going on. Tell me, Mr. Mason, is Aunt Adelle out yet? Have you been able to fix things up?'"

Mason lighted a cigarette. "I have some bad news for you, Eva. I'm not going to beat around the bush because there isn't time. I'm going to hand it to you straight from the shoulder."

Her face showed tension, but her eyes were unflinching. "Go ahead," she said.

"Police have what *seems* to be a dead-open-and-shut case against Adelle Winters."

"For . . . you mean . . ."

"For murder and theft."

"Theft?"

"Or perhaps robbery. You remember the well-filled wallet that Hines had, from which he took the bills with which he paid you?"

She nodded.

"Police found that wallet in Adelle's possession when the matron searched her at the jail. There was something over three thousand dollars in currency left in it."

"Why, Mr. Mason, that's incredible! She couldn't have taken it. Why, she'd have told me something about it if—"

"She took it all right," Mason said. "She told me so."

"When?"

"Just a short time ago. When she told me she went back upstairs to get the gun, she found the wallet lying on the floor there in the living room. Presumably Hines must have been dead in the bedroom right then, with his murderer crouching beside the body."

"Without a gun?"

"Without the murder weapon, anyway."

"Mr. Mason, I can't believe it!"

"*You* can't believe it! What do you think a jury's going to do?"

"I . . . I don't know."

"Well," Mason said, "that leaves you right in the middle

of a mess. I tried to patch things up with the district attorney's office and ran up against a brick wall. They're laying for you."

"As an accomplice?"

"As being mixed up in the whole business, along with Adelle Winters."

"But I didn't know a thing about it!"

"You signed an affidavit that contained a false statement."

"Well, I . . . I didn't see any reason for them to . . . *You* know how it was, Mr. Mason!"

"You remember that, when you discovered the body, you telephoned to me at my office and asked me to come out there?"

"Yes."

"At that time, where was your Aunt Adelle?"

"Right there."

"In the room with you—the living room of the apartment?"

"Yes."

"And where was the body?"

"In the bedroom."

"Now what was your Aunt Adelle doing while you were telephoning to me?"

"She—let's see—she went over and examined the body to make certain the man was dead."

"And while she was doing that, she could very well have lifted the wallet from the inside breast pocket of the coat, where she knew he carried it."

"Mr. Mason, Aunt Adelle wouldn't do anything like *that!*"

"But she *could* have done it."

"She wouldn't have."

"She *could* have done it?"

"Yes. She *could*. She had the opportunity, but she simply wouldn't do that."

"Well, Hines was killed with her gun. His wallet with

something over three thousand dollars in it was found in her possession. The D.A. could even make out a case of deliberate robbery, during which the victim had resisted and been shot. It's a mess, and you're mixed in it. The D.A. has given me until twelve o'clock to turn you in. I'm sorry, Eva, but I'm going to have to do it."

"Anything you say, Mr. Mason."

"I tried to do a little bargaining with the D.A.'s office. Ordinarily there would have been nothing to it, but this time Gulling, with this new evidence making him feel he's sitting on top of the world, slapped my proposition right back in my face and gave me until noon to have you at police headquarters. I'm sorry, but he holds the trumps right now. You take a cab—no later than eleven-thirty—and drive to police headquarters and give yourself up. Say I told you to do it. Don't answer any questions. Particularly, don't tell them where you were last night. Can you do that?"

"Yes."

"Be sure not to talk. Don't answer any questions about the crime—no matter how simple they sound. Understand?"

"Yes," she repeated.

"A lot of people will tell you I've given you the wrong advice, that I've put your head into a noose. But you've got to have enough confidence in me so that—even if you get the idea I'm playing the thing the wrong way—you'll abide by what I've told you. Can you do that?"

"Yes," Eva said a third time.

"Good girl! Now I'm on my way. Is there a phone here?"

"There's a booth at the back of the hall downstairs."

"Thanks—I'll call from there. Be sure you have a cab here by eleven-thirty, and get to police headquarters before twelve. I'll see you shortly after you're booked. Keep a stiff upper lip!"

On reaching the telephone booth Mason dialed the number of Paul Drake's office.

"Okay, Paul," he said when he had the detective on the line. "What do you know?"

"I guess you're clairvoyant," Drake said. "That number's in the Siglet Manor apartments—Apartment 412 on the fourth floor right by the staircase, and the tenant is a woman by the name of Carlotta Tipton. As nearly as we can find out, she's something of a glamour girl who rarely leaves the apartment before eleven o'clock in the morning, pays her rent regularly, and doesn't seem to have any steady occupation, though she wears good clothes. What does that do for you, Perry? Anything?"

Mason grinned. "That," he said, "is going to do a lot for me, Paul. Pick up Della Street, have her bring her shorthand notebook and plenty of pencils, drive like hell to the Siglet Manor Apartment House, and wait for me. I'll be there just as fast as I can make it!"

12

Paul Drake pulled up at the Siglet Manor apartments just as Perry Mason swung his car around the corner. Mason parked just behind Drake's automobile.

"Well, we made it," Della Street said as the three of them formed a group on the sidewalk. "A couple of times I was a little doubtful."

Drake said, "Evidently we're ahead of the police on the thing, Perry. Carlotta Tipton doesn't seem to have had any official visitors, as far as my men can find out. There's one of the boys over there now. I'll give him the high sign. You want us to go up with you, Perry?"

"I not only want *you* to go up, but if that's one of your men, bring him along. I want witnesses."

Drake beckoned, and a man slid from behind the steering wheel of a parked car and came over to join them.

"You folks know Frank Holt?" Drake asked. "One of my operatives. Miss Street and Perry Mason, Frank." They nodded greetings, and Drake went on, "We're going up to interview Carlotta Tipton, Frank. We want you along as a witness. Keep your eyes and ears open so you can remember afterward what takes place. Let's go."

They paused at the outer door.

"What do we do?" Drake asked. "Buzz her apartment and get her to open the door, or buzz some other apartment?"

Mason said, "If you've got a key that will work this thing . . . It doesn't take much of a master key to open the outer door of a place like this."

"Have a heart, Perry!"

"Go on, Paul, open it."

Drake looked questioningly at Frank Holt. "Got a key, Frank?"

"Sure," Holt said, and promptly opened the door.

Mason told them, "I'll do the talking, and we'll all keep our hats on. That's the best way I know to impersonate an officer, and they can't pinch you for it. Let's go"

They rode up to the fourth floor, and when they had located Carlotta Tipton's apartment Mason knocked.

The sound of movement came from the other side of the door, then a noise as though something were being dragged a short distance across the floor.

The door opened. The woman who stood on the threshold drew back at the sight of the businesslike group.

"What . . . what is this?"

Mason, assuming a hard-boiled manner, pushed past her into the apartment.

Everywhere there were signs of packing. Folded clothes were laid on a davenport. An open suitcase on the floor was about half-filled. Another suitcase, closed and strapped, had evidently been dragged aside in order to enable her to open the door.

She was slightly taller than average, a smooth-skinned redhead in the late twenties. She was wearing a skirt and blouse, but had not as yet put on make-up, and there was a slightly swollen look about her eyes which might have been due either to crying or to a hangover.

Della Street promptly went to a chair by the table, unostentatiously opened her notebook, and held a pencil poised over the page.

Frank Holt, walking over to stand by the window, pulled a cigar from his pocket, thrust it into his jaw at an upturned angle, and pulled back his vest, pushing his thumbs through the armholes.

"Well, Carlotta," Mason said, "looks rather bad, doesn't it?"

"What do you mean?"

"You've lost a meal ticket."

"It isn't . . . it isn't that. I've . . . I've lost a friend."

"Suppose you tell us about it?"

"He was killed—that's all I know."

"Sweet on him?"

"He was a friend."

"Did he pay the rent?"

"No."

"I know," Mason said. "The reason you're moving out is just that you want a change of scene every so often."

She said nothing.

"Now let's get the sketch," Mason said. "Hines would take those telephone calls down here. Then what would he do?"

There was a bewildered expression in her eyes. "I never knew very much about Bob's business," Carlotta said.

"But you knew he'd get telephone calls at this number and then call someone?"

"Yes."

"Did you know who it was?"

"Not then."

"And he'd tell her to call a certain number right away?"

"Yes."

"Suppose you tell me about what happened yesterday. What do you know about the shooting?"

"Who are you?"

"My name's Mason."

"Bob was a very dear friend," she said. "He and I were going to be married. I thought a great deal of him. Then I found out he was keeping that woman."

"What woman?"

"Why, that Helen Reedley."

Mason flashed Drake a quick glance. "You mean that Robert Hines was keeping Helen Reedley?"

"Yes."

"Have you seen the papers this morning?"

"No. I was going out and get one—I don't have any delivered. I usually get my news over the radio."

"I see. Now how did you find out he was keeping Helen Reedley?"

"Well, he was acting strange for one thing, and then I found out about what was going on."

"How?"

"I found he had another apartment key—the key to another apartment right here in this house."

"Did you know the number of the apartment?"

"Yes, the number was stamped on it—Apartment 326."

"And you knew who lived there?"

"I found out by looking on the apartment directory downstairs."

"And learned that 326 was in the name of Helen Reedley?"

"Yes."

"And she was this mysterious person that Hines had been telephoning to?"

"Well, I thought there was some connection—yes."

"What happened when Hines went out? Were you supposed to transmit telephone messages to Helen?"

"No, he always left me a telephone number where I could get in touch with him at any time, and if I couldn't reach him he'd call me back every half-hour. He was very particular about that."

"And you didn't know any of the details of his business?"

"No."

"When did you find out about this key?"

"Day before yesterday."

"And what did you do?"

"Looked up the apartment and found it was in the name of Helen Reedley."

"And then asked him about it?"

"No. What good does it do to ask a man about the woman he's two-timing you with? Don't be silly!"

"What *did* you do?"

"Followed him when he went out yesterday afternoon. I

113

listened to see if he rang for the elevator. He didn't. He went down the stairs to the third floor."

"And you trailed him?"

"Yes."

"What did he do?"

"Went into that woman's apartment."

"Did he knock?"

"Yes, he knocked and waited for a while. That gave me a chance to catch up with him. I could peek down the hall through the crack when I'd opened the stairway door an inch or two."

"He got no answer?"

"No—but he went in. He took that key from his pocket, opened the door, and went in."

"What did you do then?"

She looked at him, her expression suddenly hostile. "Say," she demanded, "what business is all this of yours, anyway?"

Mason came back at her promptly. "You want to get tough, do you?"

"No—I just wondered. . . ." Just as suddenly, she seemed deflated.

"Well, what *did* you do? Please answer my question!"

"Oh—I waited a while, and then I went along and knocked on the apartment door."

"And then what?"

"There was no answer."

"Did you say anything?"

"No. I just knocked three or four times. Then when no one came to the door, I knew the answer: he was in there with that woman."

"What did you do?"

"I came back up to this apartment and started to pack. I wish now I'd made a scene, instead—I might have saved his life!"

"What time was it that he went to that apartment?"

"Just a little before two o'clock—perhaps five minutes of two."

"And then what did you do?"

"There was no reason for me to stay here. I have a friend in Denver who is very fond of me, and he has been asking me to come to Denver. I suppose we would have gotten married. I like him a lot—but I liked Bob, too."

"And when did you hear of the murder?"

"Not until last night. I heard some people talking about it in the lobby downstairs."

"And you didn't buy a paper?"

"Yes, but it wasn't in the evening papers."

"You haven't been out to get one this morning?"

"No."

"You've had breakfast?"

"Yes."

"How long ago?"

"About an hour."

"But didn't go out to buy a paper?"

"No."

"Your friend," Mason said, "was murdered in this very apartment house, yet you didn't even go out and get a paper so as to find out any details? You didn't try to learn who murdered him?"

"Helen Reedley killed him. The police know that."

"Have you ever seen Helen Reedley?"

"Yes."

"When?"

"I met them the other day in the elevator, rode down with them. I got on here at the fourth floor, and those people, Helen Reedley and the older woman—her aunt or something—got on at the third."

"And by that time you knew that Helen Reedley had beaten your time with Bob Hines?"

"Well . . . yes."

"You didn't say anything to her?"

"No."

"Looked her over pretty carefully?"

"Naturally I would."

Mason sat thoughtfully silent for a moment, studying the

woman's face. Then he said quietly, "Helen Reedley didn't mean a thing to Bob Hines except in a financial way."

"What are you saying? He had a key to her apartment. He—"

"Sure he did, but it wasn't Helen Reedley who was in the apartment. She hired Bob Hines to get her a ringer."

"What's a ringer?"

"A double—someone who could take her place in the apartment and pretend to be Helen Reedley. Bob put an ad in a trade journal that's read by actresses—an ad asking for a brunette of a certain type."

Her eyes were wide and round now. "Are you . . . Is that the truth?"

Taking his wallet out, Mason showed her the advertisement.

She read it, and handed it back. Her lips twitched; she blinked back tears for a moment; then she suddenly pillowed her head in her arms and gave herself over to hysterical sobbing.

Mason waited until she had cried for a minute or two. Then he said gently, "So you see, Carlotta, your suspicions were entirely unfounded. When you killed him in a jealous rage you had no reason, no cause. Now suppose you tell us what actually happened."

"I've told you," she said, raising a tear-stained face.

"No, you haven't. You went to that apartment and knocked. He wouldn't open the door, so you called out that you knew he was in there. He opened the door. You dashed in. He went into the bedroom, backing away from your anger, trying to explain. You saw the gun lying there on the sideboard. You were hysterical with anger. You grabbed it up and shot him!"

"Say, what are you trying to do? Frame a murder on me?

"I want you to tell the truth. If that isn't what happened, what did happen?"

"Say, why should I tell *you* everything? Why the hell

should I tell you *anything*? Who are you anyway? Are you the police?"

"Just a minute. Let's get some of this straight, anyway. After you found he was in that apartment, you didn't do anything about it?"

"I came up and packed."

"Who's this friend of yours in Denver?"

"I'd rather not mention his name."

"But I want to know who he is. I must know whether you communicated with him."

"Well . . . I . . . I talked with him by long-distance last night."

"From this apartment?"

"No, I went out and called him from a pay station."

"What's his name?"

"You can't make me tell you."

"But you did talk with him?"

"Yes."

"And asked him if it was all right for you to come?"

"Yes."

"What time was this?"

"I'm not going to tell you that."

"As a matter of fact, didn't you call him in the afternoon rather than the evening?"

"No."

"What booth did you call him from?"

"I'm not going to answer any more questions. I don't think you . . . Say, *are* you the police?"

Mason said quickly, "Look here, Carlotta, we're investigating this crime. We want to find out everything we can about it. You want the murderer of Bob Hines to be brought to justice, don't you?"

"Are you the police?"

"No. I'm a lawyer, and these two men are detectives."

"*Police* detectives?"

"What difference does that make?" Mason asked. "Are you trying to conceal information?"

"Well, I'm certainly not going to tell everything I know

117

to anybody who just walks in here and asks me. I thought you were the police."

His eye on Della Street's pencil flying over the shorthand notebook, Mason said, "I don't know what gave you that impression. We didn't say a word about being the police. I simply dropped in to ask you some questions. I told you my name was Mason. I'm Perry Mason, a lawyer."

"Oh, so *you're* Perry Mason!"

"Yes."

"And what's your interest in this?"

"I tell you I'm trying to find out who murdered Robert Hines."

"Go to the police, then," she said sullenly.

"I think I will. Your story is very interesting."

"I was a fool to spill it to you. You—you scared me."

"What were you afraid of?"

"None of your business."

"You thought we were the police, and you were afraid of the police."

She said nothing.

"Come, come," Mason said. "You've told us enough, Carlotta, so that there's nothing to be gained by trying to clam up now."

"I wish you'd get out of here," she said. "I want to finish packing. And I haven't anything to say to you."

"Carlotta, what was the first thing you saw when you went into Helen Reedley's apartment yesterday afternoon?"

"I didn't go in. I tell you I followed Bob, and . . . and I'm not going to say anything else. You can talk to me until you're black in the face—I won't give you any more information."

"But you did see him go into that apartment?"

She sat rigidly silent.

"And you knew there was a gun on the dresser?"

Again there was no answer. Carlotta Tipton sat with her lips pressed in a firm, angry line.

Mason caught Della Street's eye and said, "Well, I guess that's all of it. Come on, folks."

Silently they filed out of the apartment, leaving Carlotta Tipton regarding them sullenly from tear-swollen eyes.

Out in the corridor Drake said, "Well, Perry, what do you make of it?"

Mason grinned. "I don't make anything of it, because I don't have to make anything of it. That's up to the police."

"You think she killed him?"

"Sure she did. Get the sequence of events, Paul. Remember that Bob Hines had given Adelle Winters the number of Carlotta's apartment where he was to be called. You can see the whole scheme now. If someone phoned Helen Reedley, Adelle Winters would answer, would say Helen was in the tub or something and would call back. Then she'd relay the message to Bob Hines. He had Helen Reedley staked out some place near a telephone, and he'd relay the message to her. She'd call her friend back, and there was no way for the friend to know where Helen was calling from.

"Now, here's what must have happened yesterday afternoon. Following my instructions, Adelle Wiinters and Eva Martell left the Reedley apartment. When they got downstairs, Adelle Winters thought she ought to notify Hines that they were leaving. I hadn't told her to, but she thought it would be a good thing. She called me first to see if she could get my permission. My line was busy. She waited a while and tried again, but kept getting the busy signal. So then she called the number Hines had given her, and got no answer at all. Now, get the significance of all that. Carlotta didn't answer the telephone—the Hines number—which means that *at the very period* when Adelle Winters was waiting in the lobby, a period of five or ten minutes, *there was no one in Carlotta Tipton's apartment;* Carlotta having started to follow Robert Hines down to the Reedley apartment. She had been doing a little detective work on her own and had found out that the man she loved had a key to another apartment in the building—an apartment listed in the name of Helen Reedley."

"On the evidence you've got so far," Drake said dubiously, "you'd have a hell of a time proving she murdered him."

Mason grinned. "The district attorney will have a hell of a time proving she *didn't* murder him. He has to establish his case against Adelle Winters beyond all reasonable doubt. I may not be able to prove that it was Carlotta Tipton who pulled the trigger on that gun, but I certainly can use her to throw a reasonable doubt on my case against Adelle Winters and Eva Martell."

"You can for a fact," Drake agreed.

"And now, Paul, we've got to find Helen Reedley."

"The police have probably been looking for her," Drake said. "They seem content with the case they've got, but they'll want to get the Reedley woman just to round it out."

Frank Holt, chewing on his unlighted cigar, said matter-of-factly, "I was taking a gander around the joint while you fellows were giving the dame the works. The telephone had a clip with a memorandum pad attached to it. I swiped that pad—here it is. One of those numbers may mean something to you."

Mason looked down the list of numbers gleefully. "Paul," he said, "it's almost certaiin that *one* of these numbers is that of the hide-out where Helen Reedley was staying and receiving reports from Robert Hines. Get to work on those numbers just as fast as you can. How long will it take?"

"How many numbers are there?"

"About a dozen," Holt said.

"It's going to be a job, Perry, but I think I can get the information in—say—well, if I'm lucky, half an hour."

"I'll be at my office," Mason said. "Get the information to me there and keep shadows on Carlotta. I don't want to lose her."

13

Back in his office Mason had no more than settled himself at his desk when his phone rang.

Drake's voice had lost its characteristic drawl. "We've checked on three of those numbers, Perry."

"What did you find?"

"One of them's an apartment hotel—permanent and transient. Helen Reedley's staying there under an assumed name."

"Where are you now, Paul?"

"I'm calling from a drugstore down at Tenth and Washington."

"How far is that from the hotel where Helen Reedley is?"

"Eight or ten blocks."

"Wait there," Mason said. "I'll be right down." He hung up the telephone and grabbed his hat.

"You wanted me to call Harry Gulling?" Della Street asked.

"Not now," Mason called over his shoulder. "I'll call him when I get back."

Joining Paul Drake, Mason drove with him to the Yucca Arms Hotel.

"How's she registered?" Mason asked.

"As Genevieve Jordan."

"You're sure it's the same one?"

"Seems to be—she answers the description. We have her number, no use bothering with the desk. Just act important and go on up. We can get by."

They rode up to Apartment 50-B and Mason knocked.

"Who is it?" a woman's voice called.

"Mr. Mason."

"I . . . I think you have the wrong apartment."

"I don't."

"Who is it?"

"*Perry* Mason."

"I . . . What? I don't know you."

"We can talk back and forth through the door, or I can come in. Which would you prefer?"

"Do whatever you please," she said. "I don't know you and I'm going to call the police if you don't go away."

Raising his voice, Mason called, "When your husband put detectives on your trail, and you decided to—"

There was the sound of a bolt being hastily thrown back. The door was flung open and indignant eyes blazed at Mason. She said bitterly, "I think you have the most obnoxious personality I have ever—" She broke off as she caught sight of Paul Drake.

"Walk right in, Paul," Mason said.

"Yes, *please* do," she said sarcastically. "Any friend of Mr. Mason is always welcome, any time of the day or night! Come right in, do! Won't you stay for dinner?"

Mason and Drake entered the apartment. As Mason closed the door behind him he said, "If you'd quit playing ring-around-the-rosy with us, Mrs. Reedley, I think we'd all be better off."

"Do you indeed?"

Mason went on affably, "There's no reason why we can't be friends. You have quite a temper, and when it flares up you're savage. But I've noticed that when you realize you're licked, you dish up a smile and try some other angle. You'd have made a good lawyer."

"Oh, would I? You can't imagine how you flatter me! And what do you want now?"

"The time is past for fooling around," Mason told her. "We want the low-down now."

"You've had everything out of me you're going to get."

"Let me present Paul Drake, head of the Drake Detective Agency. He's in my employ."

"Why, how *do* you do, Mr. Drake? I'm so glad to meet you. I've heard so much about you. Do make yourself at home. I suppose you want my diary? And a list of all my friends? And how about some photographs?"

Paying no attention to her elaborately sarcastic tone, Mason said, "Of course, we *could* go about this in another way, if we had to."

"Is that blackmail?"

"You might consider it such."

"I hate blackmail."

"You hate me anyway," Mason said cheerfully, "so you may as well make a thorough job of it. Now suppose you tell me just what the score is?"

She studied him for a moment with thoughtful eyes, then suddenly smiled. "I like a fighter," she said.

Mason said nothing.

"I know," she said, "you think it's a stall. Another one of those things you were talking about. Trying a new angle when you were blocked off on something you were trying to do. But it isn't that. I've just decided to play ball."

"Wind up and pitch," Mason said.

"Well, you've met my husband?"

"Yes."

"You're a pretty good judge of character?"

"I make a stab at it."

"All right then, you know him—restless, seething internally, insanely jealous in a possessive way, arrogant, proud, dynamic, forceful, and successful."

"A rather complex array of adjectives," Mason commented.

"A complex *man*, Mr. Mason. He's successful in business because few men stand up against the initial impact, or against the steady pressure that follows. Orville has no peace within himself, and therefore people with whom he comes in contact don't have any peace either."

"I can well imagine that it might be difficult to be his wife."

"Not so difficult to be his wife," she said slowly, "as it is to break away from being that."

"Go on."

"The man fascinated me—his drive, his ceaseless desire to dominate. I'd never known anyone before quite like him. That in itself was bad for me, because I thought I had met all the types and could catalogue almost any man within the first fifteen minutes."

"Orville didn't catalogue?" Mason asked.

"Not within the first fifteen minutes."

"You've catalogued him now?"

"Yes."

"And then got tired of him?"

"I don't think so. I doubt if I was ever in love with him. I was just fascinated by his sheer drive. As every other person must be, I was jarred by that first smashing impact with his personality. He wanted me from the moment he saw me, and when he wants something he starts beating down obstacles."

"The answer, of course," Mason said, "is that you married him. All this analysis is just a post-mortem."

"No, it isn't—it's the explanation of what followed."

"What did follow?"

"Some six months ago, I really and truly fell in love—for the first time in my life, I think."

"So what did you do?"

"I made the greatest mistake a woman ever made."

"But a common one," Mason said.

She shook her head impatiently. "You don't get me at all. I'm not referring to *that*. I went to Orville and put the cards on the table. I told him I had met someone whom I cared for, that I wanted to divorce him, and that I wanted to do it on a friendly basis."

"That was a mistake?"

"Definitely. I should have gone to him and told him that

when I married him I hadn't been sure I meant to make it permanent; that now I had decided I really cared for him and was going to stay with him the rest of his life. I knew, of course, that he had other interests; you can't expect a man of his type to be a one-woman man. It's not that he didn't care for me—it was simply the challenge that other women would naturally fling at him. If I had used my head and my knowledge of his character, I could have been free."

"So you went and told him the real truth? And what happened?"

"If you knew him you could guess what would inevitably happen. I was his wife, I was his personal possession, and he didn't intend to lose me. He was the great Orville Reedley. I *must* love him. I could not love anyone else. It was a crime to think that, with the privilege of his affection, I would even consider anyone else. Well, as I said, the inevitable resulted. He suddenly showed fierce hostility against me and against the man who was threatening to deprive him of his property."

"He knew who the man was?"

Her lips came together tightly. She shook her head. "He will never know," she said. "He must never know."

"Yet, if you were asking for a divorce," Mason said, "and if you went to him and told him frankly you loved this man, it would certainly seem that he must have known who it was."

"I am not entirely stupid, Mr. Mason. I made that one mistake in dealing with him, but I didn't make the greater mistake of telling him the name of the man with whom I had fallen in love. I tried to play square with Orville, and I learned that that was just the one way you could *not* play with him. But I knew him well enough to realize the danger of divulging the other man's identity."

"The danger?" Mason asked. "Physical, you mean?"

"I don't know . . . probably not. I have no idea what sort of weapon my husband would choose, whether physical or—well, some other kind. For the man I love is vulnerable

125

on many sides. He's no Samson physically, while financially he's none too well off."

"But you do love him?"

"I certainly do! Maybe it's because I know he needs me—the mother instinct perhaps. A part of my love for him is a fierce longing to help him because he is weak and I am strong. For, as I just said, he isn't strong physically, and it's conceivable that he might—somehow—be goaded into a nervous breakdown. He is very sensitive, to things big and little. Not only to small details but to important things like injustice. Conflict makes him shrink. Because he's a thinker—even a dreamer. But he has a wonderful imagination, which gives him a vision that impels him to build for the future. Right now his finances are shaky, but I am confident that he'll eventually be a rich man—and just as confident that some day he'll be a really *great* man!"

"In short," Mason said with a smile, "and to put it in three words, you love him. And it is this man whose identity your husband has been trying to discover?"

"Trying to discover with every means in his power. Lately, as a final resource, he decided to employ detectives. When he did that, I was desperate. I doubted whether I could keep the secret very long after private detectives got started on a systematic investigation. I decided there was only one avenue of escape."

"To hire somebody to take your place?"

"More than that. I would have to establish a completely synthetic background for myself. I knew my husband was too proud to approach me directly—it was part of his plan that I should come cringing home to *him*. He thought I'd eventually have to do just that, through lack of money—as though I valued money enough to prostitute my self-respect! I would have starved before I'd go back to him!"

"You don't *look* starved," said Mason with another smile.

Paying no attention to the interruption, she went on. "When I left my husband I didn't have much money of my own. He knew it—and I knew he knew it. But I decided not to be conservative, not to dole out what little I had, spending just so much a month and watching the money dwindle gradually. So I started to . . ."

"You started to gamble."

"Yes—I gambled."

"Speculative investments, or just plain gambling?"

"Gambling—plain and fancy gambling. And I won. And then I quit. That is, I didn't leave off gambling entirely, but I quit gambling for big money. I had won a big enough stake to provide me with something to invest. I saw that there was a good market in real estate, and I started—Well, I'm not going to tell you too much about that, because I'm somewhat vulnerable myself, you see. If my husband found out what I'd been doing . . ."

"I'm not interested in your financial affairs, but I am interested in how you happened to know that your husband intended to put detectives on your trail."

She smiled. "After all, that's simple. I told you I won my money gambling—the inital stake; and then I quit for big money. When I did that, I earned the friendship and the respect of the very men I had gambled with. Because they see lots of people try to beat the game, but only a few of them do. Most people who make big money throw it all back before they're done."

"Does your husband gamble?" Mason asked.

"Yes, but not in the places I go to. He is an inveterate poker player, and he likes to play for high stakes with a select crowd—some of them professional gamblers, the sort who are honest but shrewd. Well, at a poker session he asked one of them the name of a good detective agency that he could count on to give him service and not sell out his interests to the other side. The man recommended the Interstate Investigators. And that's all there was to it—just that one question. But a friend of mine happened to be sitting in that game, and he overheard my husband. So he came to me and said he suspected that my husband intended to put detectives on my trail."

"And Hines?" Mason asked. "How did he come into it?"

"Hines," she said, "is, or rather was, a small-time gambler. He wasn't a bookie but he would place bets for you and things of that sort. I got acquainted with him through a girl friend of his in the building where I had my apartment. He would do anything for money and was fairly competent within limits."

"And you approached him with your proposition?"

"That's right. He had no idea what was behind it, knew only that I wanted to disappear for a while and to leave someone in my place while I was gone. Because Hines had an entree to the apartment house, yet wasn't actually registered there, he was ideal for my purpose. He assured me he'd have no trouble getting a brunette who could double for me so far as an ordinary physical description was concerned. If any of my friends should come to the apartment to see me—which was unlikely because I had told all my friends never to come without telephoning first—the report would be that I was out, and whoever telephoned would be told that I'd call back inside of half an hour. Then the call was reported to Hines, and he in turn called me here and told me who had called up. I would call back direct from the hotel, and the person at the other end had no way of knowing that I wasn't calling from my apartment, of course."

"How long did you intend to keep this up?" Mason asked.

"Until my husband was presented with the picture of a very discreet young woman living with a chaperone in perfect propriety, occasionally going to dinner with Bob Hines, but being very discreet about it. He would get a picture of Caesar's wife!"

"You thought your husband would fall for that?"

"I was sure he would."

"Why?"

"Because that's the way detective agencies work. I told you I had made a mistake in judging my husband's character, and I didn't mean to repeat it. What I planned to do was—after he had that picture of his wife living a rather lonely, well-chaperoned life—was to tell him I had grown tired of the separation and wanted to return to him. This would have led him to start a suit for divorce within twenty-four hours."

"Hines impressed me as being something of a small-time opportunist."

"He was."

"Perhaps not too ethical," Mason suggested.

"Well?"

"There was the chance that he would not *be* as simple as he seemed."

"Meaning precisely what, Mr. Mason?"

"Meaning that perhaps Hines may have gone through the motions of being very docile and working with you, but that all the time he was quietly making investigations of his own to find out exactly why you wanted to have someone impersonate you."

Her face showed a quick flash of some emotion that might have been fear. But her tone was casual as she said, "I don't think there was any cause for worry on that score. Hines was rather docile so long as he was getting money."

Mason grinned. "You didn't do that very well, Mrs. Reedley."

"What do you mean?"

"That shot about Hines hit you right where you lived."

"Not at all—I had considered that possibility before I hired him!"

"Then, of course," Mason went on musingly, "having found the answer, the man certainly would not be above blackmail. That was a pretty big sum of cash money he had in his wallet, when you consider his rather small-time activities."

"How much was it?" she asked.

"A little over three thousand dollars."

"Bosh! I told you the man was a gambler, and gamblers

keep their money where it is instantly available. I know several who habitually carry ten times that amount with them."

Mason seemed to ignore her protest. "It's an interesting thought," he was saying. "Hines would start snooping around on this investigation of his own. And, knowing exactly where you were, he would be in a position to get information that the detectives wouldn't readily uncover. Then he could either sell out to your husband or threaten you with a sell-out and see how much it was worth to you to buy his silence."

"Mr. Mason, I wouldn't have paid a dime to a blackmailer!"

"What would you do?"

"I'd . . . why, I'd . . ."

"Exactly," Mason said; "you'd kill him first."

"Mr. Mason, are you insinuating that I shot Robert Hines?" she exclaimed indignantly.

"I'm verbally exploring certain very definite possibilities," he replied. "You might say I'm prospecting."

"That's hardly the way to reciprocate my frankness."

"I'm wondering just what prompted that frankness."

"Surely, Mr. Mason, you can gauge character well enough to realize what prompted it. It was a tribute to your intelligence, the mental and moral pressure you exert on people, your ability to wear down resistance. You've already noticed that I'll fight for a while, and then, when I yield, I yield suddenly and with good grace, and then come all the way, as though I had thought of some other scheme I intended to try."

Mason nodded.

"But perhaps it's a little more than that. I am intensely feminine, and there's something about you—though it is subtler—that resembles the appeal my husband had for me. There is the same initial impact of a strong personality, the same steady insistent pressure to overcome obstacles and resistance. I admire that in a man. With my husband I held

130

out for a while, then suddenly yielded. With you I have put all my cards on the table. I have been frank."

"Disconcertingly so," Mason said. "Did you have a gun in your purse when you called my office yesterday?"

"Don't be silly, Mr. Mason!"

"Did you?"

She started to say something, then looked him in the eyes. "Yes."

"What caliber?"

She hesitated. "A .38."

Mason laughed.

"You don't believe me."

"I think it was a .32," Mason said. "What did you do with it?"

"I threw it away."

"Where?"

"Where it will never be found."

"Why?"

"For obvious reasons. A man was killed in my apartment. There was every possibility I would be questioned by the police. Surely, Mr. Mason, for a man of your intelligence I don't need to fill in the details."

Mason pushed back his chair and got to his feet. "Thanks," he said, "for telling me what you did. I'm sorry I can't give you something in return. However, I might offer you a tip."

"What?"

"Ever been in you husband's apartment?"

"No."

"You know where it is?"

"Yes."

Mason said, "It's furnished in excellent taste. Only a person with very great artistic sense or a trained interior decorator could have done the job."

"Well?"

"The windows have Venetian blinds. When Paul Drake and I called on your husband we gave him a rather difficult few minutes. He wanted, perhaps, some suggestions from a friend. I noticed he walked over to one of the windows that opened on the court, and under the pretense of looking out he adjusted the blinds so that it would be possible for anyone in an apartment on the other side of the court to see in. A few minutes later the telephone rang, and your husband had an enigmatical conversation."

Her eyes were alert with interest now.

"I mentioned at the time to Paul Drake that your husband had a turbulent temperament—was constantly at war with himself. It would be strange if the decorations he had chosen for an apartment created the effect they did—of harmony, of colors perfectly combined."

"Well?" she asked.

Mason made a little gesture with his shoulders. "As you yourself must know, a gambler doesn't have to do much to give you a tip—sometimes merely the flicker of an eyelash."

Mason nodded to Paul Drake, started for the door.

She rose and walked across the room to give him her hand. "Mr. Mason," she said impulsively, "you are a very clever man and, I am afraid, a very dangerous adversary."

"Why look on me as an adversary?"

She started to say something but caught herself in time and merely smiled as she said, "I don't intend to. I was merely commenting on your potentialities. Thank you for calling, Mr. Mason. Good morning. And your friend Mr.—"

"Drake," Paul said.

"Oh yes, thank you very much, Mr. Drake, for your coöperation."

"Coöperation?" Drake asked.

She smiled. "You didn't interrupt! *Good* morning."

14

Mason entered his private office, scaled his hat at the hat rack, and said to Della Street, "Get Harry Gulling on the line as soon as you can. Then tell me what else is new."

She spun the telephone dial. "The mail came in. There are quite a few letters—two or three on top you should do something about at once."

Mason picked up the top letters and glanced at them. "Okay, I'll send a wire."

She motioned toward the telephone.

Mason picked up the instrument and said, "Hello."

Harry Gulling's voice contained no more warmth than the sound of ice cubes clinking in a frosted glass. "Good morning, Mr. Mason," he said. "I'm sorry you didn't see fit to comply with my ultimatum."

Mason jerked his watch out of his pocket. "What the devil are you talking about?" he said. "It's still three minutes till noon."

"Well?" Gulling asked.

"And my client has surrendered herself at the county jail."

"Not surrendered herself," Gulling corrected acidly. "She has been apprehended."

"What are you talking about?"

"There is, or course, rather an ingenious story," Gulling said, "which quite apparently was carefully worked out to cover the situation in case she couldn't get away. However, Mr. Mason, if you are going to gamble, you have to face the fact that gamblers often lose."

"I'm still in the dark."

"The chance you took."

"I didn't take any chance."

"Perhaps you think you didn't, but you've lost. And when a man stakes his future on a chance and loses, I'd say he was gambling. However, have it your own way."

Mason said, "I think if you'll investigate you'll find that well before twelve o'clock Eva Martell appeared at police headquarters in a taxi she herself had paid for, and surrendered herself into custody."

"She appeared at police headquarters all right, but she wasn't in a taxi. She was in the custody of a radio officer who picked her up as she was riding along the street near the apartment she shared with Cora Felton, and she was headed in the direction of the airport."

"All right—the taxicab was on its way to police headquarters."

"Sure," Gulling said. "That's what she *told* the officer, but the taxi driver doesn't say so. The cab was headed in the opposite direction."

"What *does* the driver say?"

"He picked her up and was instructed to drive down certain streets. She didn't tell him what her destination would be. Of course, that's an old dodge, telling a taxi where to turn and then—in case you're picked up—be very wide-eyed and innocent and say that you're headed for police headquarters. As far as this office is concerned, Mason, it was up to you to deliver your client before twelve o'clock. There have been too many legal flimflams in cases where you've been the attorney on the other side. We are not disposed to give you any breaks now. You had until twelve o'clock to get that girl down here. From our point of view, you didn't do it. For all we know, she may have been going to the airport."

"But that is utterly unfair!"

"It's keeping within the letter of our agreement, Mr. Mason."

"All right," Mason said angrily, "now I'll tell *you*

something. Go ahead and do whatever you damn please. I'm going to represent Eva Martell and I'm going to represent Adelle Winters, and I'll give you folks the biggest surprise you ever had."

"You mean you're going to represent Adelle Winters?" Gulling asked, unable to keep the surprise out of his voice.

"Of course I am," Mason said. "The only way I can get Eva Martell off is to be certain that the defense of Adelle Winters isn't bungled."

"She hasn't any defense."

"That's what *you* think."

"Well, Mr. Mason," Gulling said, and now his voice was purring with satisfaction, "you have an interesting record so far in murder acquittals. I don't think anything would suit this office better than to have you represent Adelle Winters. I'll be very glad to arrange things so that you can see your client any time. And as far as *your* case is concerned, I'll explain to the Grand Jury that you had an understanding with this office which you failed to keep. Incidentally, there's a woman named Mae Bagley to whom you'd better give some legal advice."

"Why?"

"She's running a rooming house at the address where the taxi driver says he picked Eva Martell up. She says she never saw Eva Martell before in her life, and never rented her a room. We're going to subpoena her before the Grand Jury. You might tell her something about the law in regard to perjury."

"That's fine," Mason said. "Get her to come to my office to ask for legal advice. If I decide I want her as a client, I'll advise her what the law *really* is."

"What do you mean by that?"

"My conception may differ from yours."

"Before you get done with this case," Gulling promised him grimly, "you'll have revised your ideas of the law as it relates to harboring a fugitive from justice."

"Prove that I harbored one," Mason challenged. "Prove

it beyond all reasonable doubt in front of a jury. And the next time, try to be a little more coöperative." And he terminated the conversation by slamming down the receiver.

He found Della Street watching him apprehensively.

"What happened, Chief?"

"Probably a stroke of luck," Mason said. "Evidently one of the radio officers who questioned Eva Martell yesterday was cruising around and happened to spot her in a taxicab. She'd made the mistake of not wanting to tell the driver to go directly to police headquarters—probably because she was a little sensitive. She told him what streets to take, evidently intending to pay him off a block or so from headquarters and walk the rest of the way. A matter of silly pride."

"But surely Gulling will understand that?"

"Gulling understands nothing except the letter of the law," Mason said. "And he's particularly anxious to put me in the position of being an accessory after the fact. His position will doubtless be that I take all technical advantage of the law and that there is no reason why the district attorney's office shouldn't do the same."

"You mean they'll actually charge you with something?"

"They may. Anyhow, they'll hold it over my head. They can't charge me with anything unless they can get some evidence to connect me with harboring Eva Martell."

"What's Eva doing?"

"Apparently she is following my instructions and saying nothing to anyone, beyond stating to the officer who arrested her that she was on her way to police headquarters to surrender."

"Won't they be able to make Mae Bagley talk?"

"She *is* talking," Mason said with a grin. "She's telling them that she never saw Eva Martell in her life, much less rented her a room!"

"But that's perjury, isn't it?"

"Not unless she makes the statment under oath," Mason

replied. "They'll have to establish that it's perjury beyond all reasonable doubt, in front of a jury. And there's a rather technical point about perjury that Mr. Gulling seems to have overlooked."

"What's that?"

"Perjury must be established by the testimony of two witnesses."

"Do you suppose Mae Bagley knows that, Chief?"

There was a twinkle in Mason's eye. "She may know *something* about the law of perjury. . . ."

"What was she charged with when you defended her and got her off, Chief?"

Mason lit a cigarette and closed one eye in a slow wink.

"Perjury," he said.

15

Monday morning's paper was interesting Perry Mason a good deal. Sitting in his office, he had it spread on the desk before him, and he was carefully reading the long and startlingly headlined story on the front page. It ran:

"WOMEN ACCUSED OF HINES MURDER TO BE DEFENDED BY PERRY MASON

Legal Wizard To Defend Both Adelle Winters and Eva Martell—D.A.'s Office Seeks To Link Lawyer with Conceal- ment of His Client

Developments in connection with the murder of Robert Dover Hines were whizzing along with bewil- dering rapidity over the weekend. Perry Mason, the noted criminal lawyer whose successes have made his name almost a household word, has announced that he is defending both Adelle Winters and Eva Martell. The retort of the district attorney's office to this was to rush Miss Mae Bagley, a rooming-house manager, before a night session of the Grand Jury. The police claim that on the night of the murder Perry Mason managed to whisk Eva Martell out from under their noses and keep her in concealment until after she had been thoroughly coached by someone in what to say, or rather in what not to say.

Mae Bagley, it is understood, cheerfully told the Grand Jury all that she didn't know. She was, she insisted, running a respectable rooming house and conforming with all the legal requirements. She had with all the legal requirements. She had never seen Eva Martell in her life, much less rented her a room.

Confronted with the fact that the driver of the taxicab in which Eva Martell was riding says that he was summoned to the rooming house operated by Mae Bagley and that he there picked up Eva Martell who was riding in his cab when police made the arrest, Miss Bagley has a whole fistful of explanations, starting with the simple statement that the taxi driver is mistaken. She points out that there are several rooming houses in the immediate vicinity, and that anyone can easily summon a taxi to go to a certain address and then be standing there in the doorway when it drives up, even if that isn't where he actually lives. She ventured a wager with the Grand Jury that she herself could summon a taxicab to call for her at the home of the assistant district attorney, could appear at his front door at the exact moment the taxicab arrived, and could—by walking down to the cab and drawing on her gloves as she left the door—create in the driver's mind the impression that she had stayed there all night—an experience which, Mae Bagley forcefully pointed out, she had no intention of enjoying.

It was rumored that her testimony brought smiles to the faces of many of the grand jurors, and that Harry Gulling, who has been in charge of mapping strategy in the case for the D.A.'s office, was plainly nettled at the answers he received. Threats of a prosecution for perjury are said to have been repeatedly made without having the slightest effect on the witness.

So far as the case against the two principal defendants is concerned, Gulling points out dryly that, according to Eva Martell's sworn statement, she was with Adelle Winters every minute of the day on which the shooting concededly occurred. Robert Hines was killed, Gulling points out, with a gun concededly owned by Adelle Winters—a gun which, according to an eye-witness, Mrs. Winters endeavored to conceal in a garbage pail at a downtown hotel shortly after the shooting. At the time of her arrest, she was found to have Hines's wallet on her person, and the murder concededly was committed in an apartment occupied at the time by Adelle Winters. If, Gulling points out, Perry Mason can find some explanation for those facts consistent with the innocence of his clients, "we might," to quote the assistant district attorney, "just as well throw the law books away, give Perry Mason the keys to the jail, and provide his clients with hunting licenses good for at least one victim a day."

There is no secret among courthouse attachés that this is something of a grudge fight of long standing. Gulling, who is recognized by those who know their way around as the mainspring in actuating strategy in the district attorney's office, is out to get Perry Mason. While Gulling seldom appears in court, he is reputed among attorneys to have a keen, methodical mind and an encyclopedic knowledge of the law.

Both prosecution and defense have signified their desire to have an early trial, and it is understood that a date left open by the continuance of another case has been tentatively suggested by Gulling, who is particularly anxious to get the murder cases disposed of so that an attempt to prosecute Perry Mason will have no legal obstacles to hurdle. It has been suggested further . . ."

Mason didn't bother to turn to the inside page. He folded the paper, tossed it to one side, and said to Della Street, "Della, I have a letter I want you to write."

She whipped open her notebook and held her pencil ready.

"This letter," Mason instructed her, "is not to be typed. It must be written in longhand on a delicately perfumed sheet of stationery. It will read: 'Dear Mr. Mason. I hope you won't think I did wrong in telling the Grand Jury I had never seen Eva Martell in my life. Things happened so fast I didn't have any time to get in touch with you and wasn't sure just what I should do under the circumstances. However, I remembered that when I last heard from you, you told me that you wanted me to put her in a room where— But I guess I'd better say this in our code.' "

Della Street looked up with surprise, her eyebrows raised interrogatively.

"Now," Mason said, "let's devise a code that no one can decipher!"

"I thought experts could decipher any code."

"They can," Mason answered with a grin, "provided the code means anything! You, Della, will fill in the rest of that sheet of social stationery with letters and numbers, all mixed together and broken up into words containing five characters each. See that there are both numbers and letters in each word. And when you finish it, sign the letter 'Mae' and bring it in to me."

"No last name?"

"No last name—just 'Mae.' "

"Chief, what in the world are you doing? It's manufacturing evidence that will put your neck in a noose!"

"Exactly," Mason said. "When you have written the letter, go to the bank and get me seven hundred and fifty dollars in cash. And," he warned as Della started for the door, "be sure to see that the handwriting in the letter is unmistakably feminine."

"Any particular type of stationery?" Della asked.

"I think Mae would buy a box of pale-rose or something of that sort; and don't forget the perfume!"

"I won't," she promised. "I'll get started right now." And she left the office.

A few minutes later Paul Drake's code knock sounded on the door of Mason's private office. The lawyer crossed over to open it.

"Hello, Paul, what's new?"

"Lots of things," Drake said. "When I got to my office I found a collection of stuff."

"Important?"

"I think it's damned important, Perry."

Drake crossed over to the big overstuffed chair, slid into his favorite position, his legs dangling over one of the arms, his back propped against the other.

"Now here's a funny one," Drake said. "I got this right from headquarters and I'm darned if I know what it means."

"Shoot."

"You know that the banks these days are quietly keeping a record of all large bills passed out. They don't say much about it, but when a man asks for big bills the bank keeps a record. Not ostentatiously, of course. For instance, the hundred-dollar bills in a drawer are listed by their serial numbers. A man who wants ten hundred-dollar bills gets the top ten—and after he's left the bank the cashier makes a note of the top ten numbers on the list, and that's that. They've got a record of who has those particular bills."

Mason nodded.

"Now in that wallet of Hines's," Drake went on, "there were twenty-one hundred-dollar bills. I don't think the police have yet traced the history of those bills, and probably they never will, because the bills came from various sources. But the point is that five of them, Perry, came from Orville L. Reedley."

"The devil they did!"

"Uh-huh."

"Well," Mason commented, "when you stop to figure that angle of it, I guess . . . Say, Paul, let's check up on this Reedley boy. Let's find out where *he* was at the time the murder was committed. After all, you know, he's supposed to be insanely jealous and—"

"He's absolutely in the clear. Police have already checked on him up one side and down the other. He had lunch that day with the local manager at the Interstate outfit. He went back to the office with this manager and was there until around two-thirty, blocking out a strategy by which he hoped to trap his wife. Incidentally, Perry, I think the guy had begun to smell a rat. I think Helen Reedley was having

142

her double put on *too* good of an act. That chaperone business was too good to be true."

Mason said, "Well, there must have been *some* connection between Hines and Reedley."

"That's what the police figure. They're giving Reedley a shakedown. As soon as they get done, I'll find out just what they've discovered."

"But why should Orville Reedley pay money to Hines? There's only one answer to that, Paul: it must have been because Hines was giving Helen Reedley a double-cross. But there's no evidence of that. There's— Wait a minute, Paul, I've got it!"

"What?"

"Don't you remember? Reedley's a gambler. He's been doing a little gambling, and it was at a poker game that he broached the subject of the detective agency. Well, Hines also is a gambler. Hang it, Paul, Hines *must* have been sitting in on that poker game when Reedley asked that question. And yet Reedley isn't supposed to know Hines . . . That money must have changed hands in a poker game and found its way into Hines's pocket."

"How?" Drake asked.

"Wait a minute," Mason said. "I'm beginning to get the picture now. That gambler friend of Helen Reedley's . . ."

"What about him?"

"Probably in love with her. Remember that Helen got Hines to rig up the double for her, but she didn't tell him why. The gambler tipped Helen off to the probability that her husband's detectives were going to be on the job, but he also wanted to know why. So he probably hired Hines to do a little snooping for *him*, and the money with which he paid Hines was, ironically enough, money that had been lost to him in a poker game—lost by Orville Reedley!"

Drake nodded. "That does it, all right, Perry. When you stop to think, it's logical enough."

"That's probably the way it was. When did Reedley get those bills at his bank?"

"About a week ago. Went in and cashed a check for five

thousand dollars—wanted it all in hundreds. The bank has a pretty good idea what he does with it. Of course, the explanation of the listing of the numbers is that the Government is trying to get information about the black market, and about the boys who are evading the income tax. Reedley has a clear record. But the bank took the numbers of those bills simply because the drawer with the hundred-dollar bills in it had already been arranged and the list was right there. So that's it, Perry."

Mason nodded in assent, but Drake had not quite finished.

"Now," Paul went on, "let's give the police a run-around on this. Orville Reedley can't tell them how Hines got those bills, because in the first place he doesn't know, and in the second he'd be afraid to even if he did know."

"Why afraid?"

"He lost them gambling," Paul explained. "Suppose he tells the officers that. Then the officers say, 'O.K., who were you gambling with? Give us the names.'"

"Boys who start tattling on these big gamblers," Mason said, "aren't very good life-insurance risks."

Drake nodded.

"So," Mason went on, "you're quite right. We'll give Orville L. Reedley to the police as a nice red herring. You say his present flame is Daphne Gridley?"

"As nearly as we can tell."

"See that the cops get a tip on that, too."

"You've already sent his wife off on a hot scent."

Mason grinned. "Start the cops on it as well. The success of a red herring, Paul, depends on choosing one who just *might* be suspect—"

"Okay, Perry, we'll toss Reedley to the wolves."

"What else have you got?"

"I don't suppose it makes any difference, but I've identified that boy friend of Helen Reedley's that she was so touchy about."

"Who is he?"

"Chap by the name of Arthur Clovis."

"How in the world did you get a line on him, Paul?"

"Through those telephone numbers on the pad that Frank Holt picked up."

"Say, wait a minute, Paul. You say the number was on that pad?"

"That's right."

"And that pad was in Carlotta Tipton's apartment?"

"Uh-huh."

"By the telephone that Hines used?"

"Yes."

"But Hines wasn't supposed to know anything about the boy friend. That was supposed to be a secret from him!"

"That's the way I understood it, too—but the number was there."

"How did you know it was Helen's friend's number?"

"We had a lucky break there. I had my men checking up on all the telephone numbers on that pad. One of them happened to be working today on this Arthur Clovis—at Clovis's apartment—when suddenly Helen Reedley came to call on Clovis. The operative who was there had no idea who she was, naturally, but he gave me a description of her a little while ago that checked out right."

"Better watch those descriptions, Paul," Mason said. "Don't forget how easy it is to find brunettes of that same physical description."

"I know, but the Reedley girl has something else that sticks out like a sore thumb. The operative made a note in parentheses after the description—he called her 'high-voltage,' That's certainly Helen Reedley."

Mason nodded. "Sounds that way. Now how about Arthur Clovis? What does he do?"

Drake grinned as he fished a cigarette case out of his pocket. "You'll get a real kick out of this, Perry."

"Okay, let me have it. What does he do?"

"He works in a bank."

"What bank?"

Drake lit the cigarette and blew out the match deliberately. "The bank where Orville L. Reedley keeps his account."

"Well, I'll be damned! What job?"

"Assistant cashier. Evidently a nice chap—dreamy-eyed and idealistic. From all we can find out, he's been saving some money and planning to go into business for himself."

"Then he's quite well acquainted with Orville Reedley?"

"I should suppose so."

"Probably handles his deposits, cashes his checks, and all that?"

"Uh-huh."

"Say, wait a minute, Paul. Do you suppose he's the one that cashed Reedley's check and recorded the numbers on those hundred-dollar bills?"

"Gosh, Perry, he may have been."

Mason frowned. "Let's give this some thought, Paul. If Hines had Arthur Clovis's phone number, it must mean he's been doing some gumshoeing of his own. Ostensibly, he was just a nice, coöperative little tool for Helen Reedley. Really, he was laying the foundation for a sell-out. He must have got that telephone number by snooping around Helen Reedley's apartment. And that gives us a picture. Helen Reedley gave him her keys and the run of the apartment, so that he could fix up this substitute brunette convincingly. He used the keys to prowl around whenever the apartment was unoccupied.

"That means only one thing, Paul—blackmail. Or a sellout, if you look at it from the other angle. Now that gambler, let's suppose he's in love with Helen Reedley. Any idea who he might be?"

"Hines went around some with Carl Orcutt," Drake replied. "Orcutt used him for little things."

"Check on Orcutt, Paul."

"That'll be tough. My operatives won't want to work on him. The guy's pretty hard, Perry. Anybody that gets in his way is likely to become a casualty."

"Well, see what you can do. And how about Helen

146

Reedley's calling on Clovis today? Why wasn't he on his job at the bank?"

"Oh, he isn't working today—he's at home, sick. Probably all broken up over the way things are going for Mrs. Reedley."

Mason got up and started to pace the floor. "Hang it, Paul, this begins to have ramifications. Why *should* Arthur Clovis be broken up?"

"Well, we've heard how sensitive he is, you know. And—after all—the bird was killed in Helen Reedley's apartment."

"Sensitive or not, Clovis must be a pretty good egg, or Helen wouldn't have fallen for him. I'd guess that he would be willing to take the gaff if he had to."

"Yes," Drake said. "You might be right, at that."

"Your man didn't have much of a talk with him?" asked Mason.

"No talk at all—didn't even see him. Didn't have to, as it turned out. He was going to represent himself as coming from an insurance company to check on a policy application Clovis had made. But when he got to the house—But first let me tell you about the house. It's one of those with no attendant in the lobby—just a whole string of bells in the vestibule. You ring the apartment you want, and a buzz signal opens the door and tells you to come up. And there's a speaking tube in case the person upstairs wants to find out who it is, before buzzing the door open.

"Well, my man had planned to snoop around the apartment house for a while, get a line perhaps on how long Clovis had been there, and even see him if he could get in. But as he was standing there in the vestibule, checking up on the address and making sure that Clovis did live there, this woman came hurrying in from the street and jabbed her finger on Clovis's bell. She gave it a short push, a long one, and then two more short ones. The buzzer sounded right away and she went on in. He got a pretty good description of her, and gave it to me."

"How long ago did this happen?"

"Apparently some time within the last hour or so. He reported just before I came up here."

Mason was silent for a few moments as he paced the floor, deep in thought. Then he said, "The thing just doesn't click, Paul. There's something wrong somewhere, some discrepancy in character. . . . Of course, no one checks the accuracy of the lists turned in by the bank employees."

"You mean the lists of serial numbers?"

"That's right. A cashier's cash has to balance at the end of the day; but he can take out all the hundred-dollar bills he wants, make up the amount with twenties, and report giving hundred-dollar bills to anyone."

"You mean that those hundred-dollar bills that Hines had *didn't* come to him through the husband?"

"I don't know," Mason said. "But when the assistant bank cashier who has reported giving hundred-dollar bills to a husband turns out to be the boy friend of the husband's estranged wife, and those bills show up in the wallet of a man who was murdered in the wife's apartment—well, after all, Paul . . . it does make me skeptical."

"Hell," Drake said, "when you put it that way, it makes me skeptical, too! Let's go see the guy."

Mason nodded. "I want to wait for Della. She's gone down to pick up some cash."

"Not in hundred-dollar bills, I hope?"

Mason grinned. "In hundred-dollar bills, Paul. And I only hope the bank keeps a record of them. Here she is now."

Della Street breezed into the office. "Hi, Paul! Here's the money, Chief."

"Okay, get that letter written. I'm going out with Paul. Probably back in three-quarters of an hour."

"Rumor around the courthouse is that Harry Gulling is laying for you, Perry."

"Let him lay," Mason said. "He *may* lay an egg."

16

Mason pushed the button opposite the name ARTHUR CLOVIS, giving a short ring, then a long, and then two shorts. Almostly instantly the buzzing of the door signified that the electrically controlled catch had been released and Drake, who was waiting, pushed the door open.

"What's the number?" Mason asked.

"Two-eleven."

"An elevator?"

"I don't know. But here are the stairs, anyhow."

"Okay, we'll walk up," Mason said.

They climbed to the second floor, found the apartment they wanted, and Mason tapped gently.

The door was flung open. A man's voice said, "Why, Helen, what brings you back—" He stopped in open-mouthed astonishment.

Mason thrust out his hand, his smile was affable. "Mr. Clovis, I believe?"

"That's right."

"My name's Mason, and this is Mr. Drake. May we come in?" And Mason pushed on past the startled young man, seated himself, smiled, and said, "I was talking with Helen Reedley. I believe she told you about it."

"She . . . Did she send you here?"

Mason's face showed surprise. "You mean you didn't know I was coming?"

"No."

"Well, close the door and sit down; we may as well talk things over without taking the whole apartment house into our confidence. I want to find out what you can tell me about what happened when Orville Reedley cashed that five-thousand-dollar check. I believe you were the one who took the record of the numbers. . . ."

Arthur Clovis's face showed relief. "Oh, *that*. That's all been taken care of. A Lieutenant Tragg from the Homicide Division of the Metropolitan Police force questioned me and drew up a written statement for me to sign."

"You cashed the check for Reedley?"

"Yes, I did."

"Worked in the bank for some time, have you?"

"Three or four years."

"Know Orville Reedley quite well?"

"Only as a depositor."

"Wait on him frequently?"

"Yes. As it happens, I'm in charge of the window R-to-Z and I often have dealings with Mr. Reedley."

"Large cash withdrawals?"

"I'm afraid I'm not allowed to discuss the affairs of a client at the bank. But if you'll get in touch with the account manager, he'll doubtless—"

"I'll do that later," Mason interrupted. "I'm interested now in finding out something of the personal relationship."

"What do you mean?"

"You're in love with Reedley's wife."

"Mr. Mason!"

"Come, come," Mason said, "save the dramatics. Let's just get down to brass tacks."

"That remark is . . ."

"The truth," Mason finished, as Clovis hesitated.

"You are asking about something that is none of your business. Damn your impertinence anyway!"

"Let's skip all this, Clovis, and find out what the score is. The last thing you want is to have this given any publicity. And, what's more to the point, you know very well that it's the last thing Helen wants. I have all the facts, so let's not do any bluffing. We can save time being frank."

"I understand you are an attorney," Clovis said sullenly.

"That's right."

"Well, what business is this of yours?"

"I'm making an investigation on behalf of my clients."

"Who are your clients?"

"Two women, Adelle Winters and Eva Martell. Do you know them?"

"No."

"Then you shouldn't have any hesitancy about answering questions."

"It's a matter I don't care to discuss."

"If necessary, I can subpoena you as a witness at the preliminary examination, put you on the stand, and get the information I want in front of a courtroom full of people."

"I don't think the law would let you do that."

Mason lit a cigarette and said nonchalantly, "Lots of people disagree with me about points of law. Some of them are lawyers, too."

"Just what do you want to know?"

"I want to know what the set-up is. I want to know why Helen Reedley arranged for a stand-in. I want to know why you're so surreptitious about your affair with Helen."

"Helen is a married woman, and there's no 'affair.'"

"She's left her husband."

"Who is a particularly ruthless, determined man, unusually possessive and jealous."

"And so you're afraid of him?"

"Afraid of him?" Clovis exclaimed indignantly. "Hell, I've been wanting to go have it out with him for two months, but I refrained on account of Helen. She's frightened to death of him. He has all but ruined her life. She's becoming a nervous wreck."

"Did you know about the woman who was impersonating Helen Reedley?"

"No."

"You knew Helen wasn't at her apartment."

"She told me she'd let a friend have the apartment."

"And gave you her new address at the hotel?"

"Yes."

"You saw her there?"

"Yes."

"Went out with her?"

"Yes."

"Same old restaurants as usual?"

Clovis started to say "Yes," then gave the question puzzled consideration, changed his mind, and said, "Well no, as a matter of fact, we were going to new restaurants."

"I know," Mason said, "but you didn't have any idea of the purpose back of all this?"

"None whatever."

"Until Hines came to see you," Mason said.

Clovis jerked as though Mason had pushed a pin into him. "Hines," he said, as though the repetition of the name would give him time to think.

"He came to see you?" Mason asked.

"What makes you think he did?"

"Did he?"

"Well, yes."

"When?"

"The morning of the third."

"What did he want?"

"I . . . Mr. Mason, you won't think this is the truth, but it is. I simply don't know *what* the man wanted."

"Didn't he say?"

"No."

"Lay any foundation for meeting you at a later time under different circumstances?"

"No."

"Any attempt at blackmail?"

"I don't *think* there was."

"Why don't you *know?*"

"Because I wasn't at the time aware of all the circumstances. And in such a situation, naturally, one is likely to overlook significant passages in the conversation, little hidden meanings that tie in with . . ."

"Suppose you tell me exactly what happened."

"I was on duty at the bank. Hines came to my window. It was during a slack period and there was no queue. When he gave me his name I told him he was at the wrong window, that I handled only the R-to-Z deposits. He smiled and said, no, he thought he was at the right window."

"Then what?"

"Then he started making enigmatic remarks. I couldn't get what he was driving at."

"Can you remember what he said?"

"Well, it was all rather mysterious. He said he might want to borrow some money, and that the person who would endorse his note would be a depositor whose name would be in the accounts that were handled at my window."

"And what did you tell him?"

"I told him that notes were handled in an entirely different department in the bank. And then he asked, 'I suppose you know Orville L. Reedley and Helen Reedley, his wife?' I didn't answer the question directly, though I was perfectly polite—I just told him he would have to inquire at the Loan Department."

"Then what happened?"

"He started to turn away from the window, then stopped and smiled pleasantly and said, 'I've seen your face before,' or something of that sort. I told him I didn't remember him and he said that he had a girl friend who lived in the Siglet Manor Apartments and asked me if I knew the place."

"What did you do?" Mason asked.

"I simply turned away. He smiled and walked out."

"Do you know whether he went to the Loan Department?"

"No, he didn't—he just walked out. I watched him."

"He intimated to you that he would be asking to borrow money on a note signed by Helen Reedley?"

"Or Orville Reedley. That, or course, was just my guess. I don't really *know*."

"I understand. There was no suggestion of blackmail?"

"Blackmail? Well—no. Only the smirking, insinuating way he approached me."

"Was it threatening?"

"Not threat so much as unctuous assurance."

"And what are you going to do, now that the cat's out of the bag?"

"Going to do?" Clovis exclaimed. "I'm going to see Orville Reedley and tell him that he can't ruin Helen's life by arbitrarily refusing her a divorce. She doesn't need his consent, really. It might not be pleasant—it might be . . . To hell with it! I'll fight. *I'm* not going to be pushed around."

"Are you absolutely certain that Hines didn't cash a check?"

"When?"

"When he called at the bank."

"Hines cash a check? Absolutely not! Not at my window. He couldn't have cashed it there anyhow, because I don't have any H clients. But from the way he talked I don't think he had any money in the bank. I didn't check to find out, but I don't think he has a dime with us."

"You're sure you didn't give him five hundred dollars, and then tell the police that the five hundred had been delivered to Orville Reedley on a check *he* had cashed?"

"Mr. Mason—please! What on earth gave you any such idea as that?"

"I don't know," Mason said, and added somewhat wryly, "And I wish I did. Does Mrs. Reedley know you plan to talk with her husband?"

"I told her I was going to."

"What did she say?"

"She pleaded with me not to. She said that would spill the beans; that her husband would never consent to a divorce and that we would have played right into his hand."

"Look here," Mason said. "Did you ever, under any circumstances or for any length of time, have a key to Helen Reedley's apartment?"

"Hang it, Mason, that's a slanderous insinuation! You can't—"

"Keep your shirt on. Answer my question. Did you at any time have a key to Helen Reedley's apartment?"

"No."

"Not for any period of time, no matter how brief? Not just to go and get something for her?"

"No!"

Mason said, "Hines had a key."

"He was working for her. He had to go in and out."

"And you never had a key, not even for a brief period? She never sent you up there to get something for her?"

"Absolutely not! If Helen had wanted anything in her apartment, she'd have got it herself. She would never have thought of sending me up there with a key."

"I'm trying to get certain points cleared up. There doesn't seem to be any pattern yet, and I'm trying to get the real facts. I was hoping you could help me."

"I can tell you this much: Orville Reedley is intensely jealous and possessive—absolutely impossible! He refused to give his wife a divorce and swore that he'd contest any divorce she'd apply for. She had placed herself in his power by telling him that she cared for someone else."

"Any witnesses to that conversation?"

"No—there were just the two of them. But that's one thing about Helen Reedley, she wouldn't lie for anybody; she wouldn't even shade the truth. If her husband ever got on the witness stand and repeated that conversation, Helen wouldn't deny it—she isn't built that way. You can bank on that: Helen won't lie!"

Mason was silent for a moment. Then he said, "You were on duty at the bank when Hines showed up and talked with you?"

Clovis nodded.

"That was the day of the murder?"

"That's right."

"You saw Helen Reedley that same day?"

"Yes, she was in the cafeteria where I usually eat lunch."

"What time?"

"Twelve-thirty."

"You knew she'd be there?"

"Well, I . . .."

"You've seen her there before?"

"Yes."

"Sat at the same table with her?"

"Well, naturally."

"You told her about Hines?"

"Yes."

"And then what happened?"

"Why, we ate lunch—that's all."

"Did she say anything to lead you to believe she was at all concerned over the conversation you'd had with Hines?"

"Not exactly. She said she knew him slightly."

"And what time did you leave her?"

"Well, it was about—oh, I'd say a little after one-thirty."

"A little *after* one-thirty?"

"Yes."

"I thought you said you had lunch at twelve-thirty?"

"I did."

"Do you have more than an hour for lunch?"

"Well, I . . . I wasn't feeling well that afternoon and took the rest of the day off. I had one of my headaches—eyestrain."

"Now then," Mason said, "tell me the truth, because I can verify it by checking up on your record at the bank. How many days have you missed work in the last six months because of those headaches?"

Clovis hesitated.

"Come on," Mason said, "let's be frank. How many days?"

"The afternoon of the third—and today."

"You've had a hundred-percent record at the bank up until the day Hines was murdered?"

"Why keep referring to it as the day the man was murdered? It was the third of this month!"

"All right, we'll call it the third. Where did Helen Reedley go when she left the cafeteria on the third?"

"I don't know."

"Did you *try* to follow her?"

"Mr. Mason, I've been patient with you and answered a lot of questions about matters that are really none of your business, if I may say so. Now I am going to ask you and your companion to leave. Really—I'm too nervous to answer any further questions."

"Then I am to assume that you *did* try to follow her?"

"Mr. Mason, will you please leave this apartment?"

Mason nodded to Paul Drake. "I guess that's as good as we want," he said. The two men walked across to the door. Just before Mason stepped out into the corridor, he turned and shot a rapid-fire question at Arthur Clovis. "Did you follow her *all* the way to the Siglet Manor Apartments?"

In dignified silence, Clovis walked over and closed the door behind him.

"Well," Mason said out in the corridor, "that's that!"

"What do you make of it, Perry?"

"Darned if I know," Mason said. "He's trying to cover for her, for *something*. He knows something that has him worried sick—Lord knows what it is. He's no weak sister, but he's certainly a nonbelligerent! A high-voltage girl like Helen Reedley would fall for the big, dynamic type, and then on the rebound—as her mother instinct came to the fore—she'd fall for some clean-cut young chap who is sensitive, shy, and retiring, but has a nice clean mind and a healthy imagination."

"Meaning Arthur Clovis?"

"Arthur Clovis comes pretty close to answering that description."

"So what do we do?" Drake asked.

"We go back and wait for something to break. We've stretched several wires almost to the breaking point. What I want right now is to have something crack that will give Gulling a jolt. He's going to get me before the Grand Jury. I want to have this preliminary hearing slap him in the face with a surprise before he gets me there."

17

In those tense few moments before the arrival of the judge on the bench, the whispered comments of the spectators sounded like a continual hissing. What came as considerable surprise to the initiate was the fact that Harry Gulling was present personally at this preliminary hearing, representing the district attorney's office and thus advertising to those who knew their way around the courthouse that this was indeed the "grudge fight" it had been called in the papers.

Perry Mason looked up as a deputy sheriff brought in Adelle Winters and Eva Martell. The lawyer rose, shook hands with the two defendants, and saw that they were seated beside him.

"I'm so sorry about that taxicab," Eva Martell whispered. "I thought I would drive by the apartment that Cora and I shared, and if the police weren't watching it . . . It was foolish—I don't know why I did it."

"That's all right," Mason said. "That's all water under the bridge now."

"They've been trying to get a statement out of me. Not so much about the crime itself as about where I stayed that night. Whether you had anything to do with getting me . . ."

"I know," Mason whispered. "Let's not bother about it. Excuse me for a moment—there's Paul Drake. I have to see him." He got up and beckoned to Drake, who had just entered the courtroom.

As the detective joined him, Mason said, "Paul, stand

close to me. I'm going to slip you something. I don't want anyone to see it."

"What?"

Mason didn't answer him directly, but said, "This is something I've been hoping for but hardly dared believe might happen: Harry Gulling is going to handle the case for the prosecution himself!"

"Isn't that rather unusual?"

"Damn near unique!" Mason replied. "As you know, he's the shrewd legal mind that guides the policy of the district attorney's office, but I never thought he'd be much good before a jury—his mind is too mathematical and detached, and he hasn't enough understanding of human nature. Now, listen, Paul: I want to have witnesses to the contents of this wallet. It's my own, and I want an inventory of it made. In it are some money, some letters, my driving license, and a few other papers. I want Gulling to find it in the men's room."

"Going to be rather difficult," Drake said.

"No, it isn't. You can have a man in there ready to plant it. Then have another man out in the corridor who can give a signal when Gulling heads that way. I want it left where it will be readily seen, but where it isn't *too* conspicuous."

"Okay," Drake said. "I'll give it a whirl."

Mason moved closer and slipped the wallet into Drake's hand. "Make sure Gulling gets it, and—"

They were interruptted by the banging of a gavel and a clerk ordering everyone to stand.

Judge Homer C. Lindale entered the courtroom, took his place at the bench, and nodded the spectators to their chairs. A moment later he called the case of The People vs. Adelle Winters and Eva Martell.

"Ready for the prosecution," Gulling said.

"Ready for the defense," Mason announced.

"Proceed," Judge Lindale said to Gulling.

"Your Honor is familiar with the crime charged?"

"I have read the complaint. It is a case of first-degree murder, I believe."

"Yes, Your Honor. The defendants are charged jointly and are both represented by Mr. Mason."

"I so understand. Proceed."

"Your Honor, my first witness will be Samuel Dixon."

Dixon, duly sworn, took the witness stand, stated that he was a radio-car officer and had been such on the third of the month when he received a call to go to Siglet Manor Apartments and investigate at Apartment 326. On arriving there he had found both defendants in the apartment. The younger, Eva Martell, was excited and somewhat hysterical, but the older one, Adelle Winters, was quite calm and collected. They had shown him a body which they said was that of a man named Robert Hines.

"Where was this body?"

"Seated in a chair in the bedroom, rather slumped forward, the head inclined over toward the right shoulder. There was a hole almost in the center of the forehead. There were powder marks visible around the hole, indicating that it was a bullet hole. There had been some hemorrhage. The man was in his shirt sleeves. His coat had been removed and hung over the back of the chair in which the body was slumped."

"Did the defendants make any statements to you in regard to the identity of the dead man or how they happened to discover him?"

"Yes, sir."

"What were those statements?"

"Signed statements?" Mason interrupted.

"The statements I am referring to at this time were not signed," Gulling said.

Mason said, "I understand, Your Honor, that the defendants signed certain statements. If that is so, the statements themselves are the best evidence."

"The statements I am now asking for are merely oral statements which were made to this witness," Gulling said.

"Objection overruled."

"May I ask if these statements are considered by the prosecution to be in the nature of admissions? Or are they confessions?"

"I fail to see that that makes any difference."

"It they aren't either one, I shall object to them as imcompetent, irrelevant, and immaterial."

"They are statements."

"Very well. Then I shall object to them on the ground that no proper foundation has been laid."

"They are not confessions, if that is what you mean. They are statements—admissions."

"Objection overruled," Judge Lindale said.

"Yes," the witness went on, "both defendants made statements. They said that they'd been employed by Mr. Hines to live in this apartment. The defendant Eva Martell said she had been instructed to take the name of Helen Reedley."

"If the Court please," Mason said, "I would like to be heard upon my objection. After all, there is no proof of the *corpus delicti* as yet. We have merely the body of a dead man. It seems that the orderly way would be to show the identity of this man and some medical testimony indicating that death was the result of violence. For all that has appeared so far, the man may have died of heart trouble."

"With a bullet in his forehead?" Gulling asked sarcastically.

"Oh," Mason said, "so there was a *bullet* in his forehead! That changes the situation."

"Yes, there was a bullet."

"I would like to cross-examine the witness about that bullet for the purpose of proving the *corpus delicti* before these other questions are asked."

"This witness didn't see the bullet," Gulling said.

"Then how did he know there was a bullet?"

"The autopsy surgeon told him so!" Gulling shouted—and then flushed before Judge Lindale's smile. He went on

161

more calmly. "Very well," he said, "I will prove the *corpus delicti*. If you will step down, Mr. Dixon, I'll ask to have Helen Reedley sworn."

With obvious reluctance Helen Reedley took the witness stand.

"Were you acquainted during his lifetime with Robert Dover Hines?" Gulling asked.

"I was."

"Did you see him on the third day of this month?"

"I did not actually see him on that date, but I talked with him."

"On the telephone?"

"Yes."

"You had, however, seen him prior to that time?"

"Many times, yes."

"You were familiar with him? You know who he was?"

"Yes, I do."

"You rented an apartment at the Siglet Manor Apartments, number 326?"

"I did, yes."

"You had given Mr. Hines permission to occupy your apartment?"

"Temporarily, yes."

"And did you on the fourth day of this month, at the request of the police, go to the morgue?"

"I did."

"And there you saw the body of a man?"

"Yes."

"Did you know that man?"

"Yes."

"Who was it?"

"Mr. Hines."

"Robert Dover Hines?"

"Yes."

"The same person to whom you had given permission to occupy your apartment?"

"Yes."

"Cross-examine," Gulling said.

"When you gave Mr. Hines permission to occupy your apartment, you gave him a key to the apartment?" Mason asked.

"Yes."

"And what was your object in giving him this key and permission to occupy the apartment?"

"Just a moment, Your Honor," Gulling said. "That is objected to as incompetent, irrelevant, immaterial, and not proper cross-examination. This witness is called purely for the purpose of establishing the identity of the deceased, and that is all."

"Then why ask her if she had given the deceased permission to occupy her apartment?" Mason asked.

"It shows why he was there."

"Exactly," Mason said. "That is what I'm trying to show— *why he was there.*"

"I didn't mean it that way, Your Honor," Gulling said.

Mason said, "I did, Your Honor."

"If the Court please," Gulling exclaimed angrily, "I don't want to have all these extraneous matters dragged into this case. If Mr. Mason has any defense he wished to produce, he is at perfect liberty to do so. But, so far as my case is concerned, I merely want to show the identity of the dead man, the manner in which he met his death, and the fact that there is more than a probability that these defendants brought about that death in a deliberate, cold-blooded manner and for the purpose of perpetrating a theft."

"Then by all means," Mason said, "the Court should know the reason why the defendants were in the apartment, and the reason why Hines was in the apartment."

"As a part of *your* case, if you want—not as a part of *mine*," Gulling snorted.

"Perhaps," Mason said, "I can clear up the situation by pointing out to the Court that the witness has been asked about the permission she gave Hines to occupy her apartment. If that permission was in writing, then the writing itself is the best evidence and should be introduced. If the permission was oral, then—under a well-established rule of law—when the prosecution introduces a *part* of a conversation I have a right to introduce it all."

Gulling was unmistakably angry now. "We'll be here all winter, Your Honor, if all these minor matters are going to be dragged into the case."

"I don't think it's exactly a minor matter," Judge Lindale ruled. "I would have said that it was part of the defendants' case, were it not that the witness has been asked about something that obviously was a conversation. I will rule that *if* this was a part of the conversation, Counsel has a right to show all of the conversation on cross-examination. I would suggest you reframe your question, Mr. Mason."

"Very well," Mason said. Turning to the witness, he smiled. "You have stated that you gave Robert Hines permission to occupy your apartment?"

"Yes, sir."

"That was in a conversation?"

"Yes, sir."

"What else was said in that conversation?"

"Your Honor, I object to that," Gulling said. "It is a blanket question—it calls for everything."

"Exactly," Mason said.

"Overruled."

"Answer the question, Mrs. Reedley."

Helen Reedley chose her words carefully, trying desperately to betray as few of the facts as possible. "I don't remember the entire conversation. We had several conversations on the subject. But at the time when I gave Mr. Hines permission to occupy my apartment—"

"And if the Court please," Gulling interrupted, "it's only that one conversation that we are interested in. Any earlier conversations or negotiations looking toward the giving of that permission must be brought out elsewhere. On cross-examination, all that may be brought out is what was said at that *one* conversation.

"That is correct so far as the present ruling of the Court is concerned," Judge Lindale said.

"Well, at that one conversation," Helen Reedley said, "I told Mr. Hines he could occupy my apartment. I gave him a key to it, and we arranged that he would relay any telephone calls to me. In other words, if any telephone calls from my friends were received at that apartment, they would be relayed to Mr. Hines, who would in turn pass them on to me."

"Anything else you can think of?" Mason asked.

"Not at *that* conversation," she said. "No."

"Any conversation about getting two women to occupy the apartment?"

"It was understood that Mr. Hines was to get someone to occupy the apartment."

"To take your place?"

"Not exactly."

"To use your name?"

"Well, yes."

Mason said, "I'll show you an advertisement that was published in a theatrical paper, and ask you if you consulted Mr. Hines about inserting it."

"In that particular conversation," Gulling amended.

"That's right—in that particular conversation."

"No, that was done by Mr. Hines without consulting me," Helen Reedley said.

"Did you, at that conversation, have some understanding with Mr. Hines as to the type of woman who was to occupy your apartment? Specifically, that she was to be a brunette with certain definite physical characteristics?"

"Well . . ."

"Yes or no?" Mason asked.

"Yes."

"What were the specifications?"

"I gave him my measurements—height, weight, waist measure, and so forth."

"Why?"

"Objected to as incompetent, irrelevant, immaterial, and not proper cross-examination," Gulling said.

Judge Lindale was now plainly interested. He was leaning forward in his chair looking at the witness. "Do I understand," he asked, "that you authorized Mr. Hines to use your apartment, that you gave him a key to your apartment, and that in addition it was arranged that he was to get a woman of your exact description to take your name and occupy your apartment?"

"Not at the conversation, if the Court please," Gulling said. "It was the result of several conversations."

"The Court wants an answer to that one question," Judge Lindale said. He sounded irritated.

"That was the general understanding," Helen Reedley admitted.

"And Mr. Mason has asked this witness *why* that understanding was reached?"

"Yes, Your Honor," Mason said.

"And that is what is objected to, if the Court please," Gulling said; "because it was an understanding reached in prior conversations and did not have anything to do with this one conversation at which permission was given to occupy the apartment. If the Court please, the loophole through which the defense attorney has squirmed to bring out this matter on cross-examination is exceedingly small— an opening based on a technicality only. I feel that the opening should not be enlarged."

"Well," Judge Lindale said, "I think that Counsel is perhaps right—technically right. But at some stage of the proceedings the Court wants to find out *why* this impersonation was permitted."

"Not an impersonation, Your Honor," Gulling said.

"Well, what was it?" Judge Lindale said.

"It was merely a subletting of the apartment."

"Humph!" Lindale snapped. "To a woman who had the physical appearance of the witness and who was to assume her name?"

"Well, yes, Your Honor."

"If that isn't an impersonation, I don't know one when I see it," Judge Lindale said. "However, the Court will limit the cross-examination to matters that were covered on direct examination. Proceed with your questions, Mr. Mason."

"Now," Mason said, "you have stated that you did not see Robert Dover Hines on the third, the day of the murder."

"Yes, sir."

"Are you certain of that?"

"Yes, sir."

"Where were you at twelve-thirty o'clock in the afternoon on that day?"

"I . . . I was at lunch."

"Alone?"

"Objected to as incompetent, irrelevant, and immaterial and not proper cross-examination," Gulling said.

Judge Lindale sighed. "Well, technically I suppose the objection may be well taken—unless it should appear that the witness lunched with the decedent Hines; and I take it, Mr. Mason, there is no contention that such was the case?"

"None, Your Honor. I merely want to follow the movements of the witness from lunch until the time of the murder. I believe that this is a sufficiently narrow field to be reasonable cross-examination of a witness who has stated she did not see the decedent on that day."

"What was the time of the murder?"

"I believe the prosecution fixes it at two o'clock."

"At between one-fifty-five and two-fifteen, Your Honor."

"Very well," said Judge Lindale. "That is a period of twenty minutes during which it is claimed that the murder was committed. I believe that an examination of this witness as to her whereabouts from twelve-thirty on is permissible in view of the fact that she has stated she did not see the decedent during the entire day of the third."

"You finished lunch at approximately one-thirty?" Mason asked.

"Yes, sir."

"And where did you go?"

"Incompetent, irrelevant, immaterial," Gullin said mechanically. "Not proper cross-examination."

"Overruled."

"I . . . I went to . . . to a certain restaurant."

"You had already had lunch," Mason said. "You went to this restaurant for the purpose of seeing someone?"

"Well, yes."

"And that person was Robert Hines?"

"Yes."

"Did you see him?"

"No."

"Did you talk with him on the telephone?"

"Earlier in the day I had talked with him on the telephone."

"After one-thirty did you talk with him on the phone?"

"No."

"Did you try to?"

"Yes."

"You called him at a number he had given you?"

"Yes."

"The number of a telephone in an apartment in the Siglet Manor Apartments—*another* apartment, that is?"

"I believe it is—yes."

"An apartment rented by Carlotta Tipton?"

"I—I believe so, yes."

"Had you ever met Carlotta Tipton?"

"Not to speak to. I had seen her once or twice. I think I had ridden up in the elevator with her."

"By the elevator, you mean the elevator of the Siglet Manor Apartments?"

"Yes."

"And when you went to this restaurant on the day of the murder looking for Robert Hines, you had reason to believe he would be at this restaurant for lunch?"

"Yes."

"Yet you made no attempt to get in touch with him until after one-thirty?"

"That's right."

"Rather late for lunch, isn't it?"

"Well . . . I was hoping that perhaps he would be there."

"Taking a chance on it?"

"If you want to put it that way, yes."

"But had you gone there earlier, you would have been *sure* to catch him, wouldn't you?"

"I . . . I suppose so."

Mason said, "Is it a fair inference that the thing that made you so anxious to get in touch with Mr. Hines was something that happened during your own luncheon engagement. Is that right?"

"Your Honor, I object," Gulling exclaimed. "That's purely a conclusion."

"Not a conclusion of the witness, but a conclusion of Counsel," Mason said smiling.

"And," Judge Lindale remarked dryly, "one that is quite obvious to the Court. Mr. Gulling, can't we proceed with the hearing without quite so many objections from Counsel? After all, this is not a matter before a jury, and it would seem that we might dispense with some of the more technical objections."

"I'll withdraw the question," Mason said. "And I have only one or two more questions to ask. Mrs. Reedley, you gave Mr. Hines some money at the time of this conversation, did you not?"

"Yes."

"In hundred-dollar bills?"

"Hundreds and fifties."

"How much?"

"Five hundred dollars."

"Had you previously received some of that money from your husband?"

Gulling said sullenly, "Your Honor, I dislike to seem

over-technical in the face of the Court's admonition, but it is obvious what Mr. Mason is doing. He has trapped me into making technical objections until the Court has requested—"

"I think Counsel is right," Judge Lindale said. "Mr. Mason, you will appreciate, of course, the necessity of coöperation by counsel on both sides. The Court has asked for fewer technical objections. That certainly means that Counsel asking the questions should lean over backwards to keep his examination within the rules of evidence, not take advantage of the condition."

"Your Honor, I appreciate that," Mason said, "and because the situation may reflect somewhat on my professional integrity, may I explain the purpose of the question?"

"Very well."

"As I understand it," Mason said, "it is the contention of the prosecution that at the time Hines was killed he had a wallet in his possession containing some three thousand dollars in currency. I understand further that the numbers on some of those bills have been traced to the husband of this witness. It therefore becomes vitally important to ascertain whether those bills found their way into that wallet as a consequence of this transaction with Mrs. Reedley, or whether they reached the wallet from some other source."

Judge Lindale's eyes showed his interest. He turned to Gulling. "Is that approximately correct, Mr. Deputy District Attorney?"

"Your Honor, I respectfully submit that this is an attempt to force the prosecution to put on its case out of order."

"Mr. Mason has made a statement explaining the reason for a question," Judge Lindale said. "I am asking if Mr. Mason's statement is approximately correct."

"The statement *is* approximately correct—but that certainly does not mean that the door can be opened so wide on cross-examination."

"Well," Judge Lindale said, "if we are going to get technical, this cross-examination may not be on any subject brought out in the direct examination; but it may go to show the bias of the witness. And if we're going to be technical, gentlemen, we'll be technical on both sides. The objection is overruled. Answer the question."

"No," Helen Reedley said. "There was not a single dollar of the money I gave Mr. Hines that I had received from my husband. I have not had any money from my husband for some six months."

"Thank you," Mason said. "That is all."

"No redirect," Gulling snapped.

"Your next witness?" Lindale asked.

"Your Honor, it becomes necessary for me to present one phase of my case slightly out of order. I wish to call one witness for just a question or two."

"Very well."

"Mr. Thomas Folsom," Gulling said, "will you come foward and be sworn?"

Tom Folsom proved to be a tall, loose-jointed man. He was sworn, took the witness stand, crossed long legs, and settled back like a person to whom the witness chair is a familiar seat.

"Your name is Thomas Folsom, and you're a private detective employed by the Interstate Investigators, and you were so employed on the third of this month and had been for some time prior to that date?"

"Yes, sir."

"I will direct your attention to the defendant Adelle Winters, and ask if you saw her on the third of the month at approximately two-twenty in the afternoon?"

"I did."

"Where?"

"At the Lorenzo Hotel."

"What was she doing?"

"At that particular time?"

"At that particular time."

"She was there with the other defendant, Eva Martell. They arrived at the hotel around a quarter past two in the afternoon. At about two-twenty, while Eva Martell was telephoning, the defendant Winters, whom *I* had been instructed to shadow, started to walk rather aimlessly around the hotel lobby. Then she went through a door marked 'Baggage Room,' and through another door that led to an alley, and finally turned down a side passageway back of the hotel dining room.''

"And what did she do there?"

"Three garbage cans were standing out there in a row. She raised the lid of the middle one, stood there briefly for a moment, apparently dropped something into it, then replaced the lid and turned back toward the main passageway.''

"This was at approximately two-twenty, and immediately afterwards?"

"Yes, sir."

"Cross-examine," Gulling snapped.

Mason said, "You were instructed to shadow the defendant Adelle Winters?"

"Yes, sir.''

"And had been shadowing her for some time before you saw her there at the hotel?"

"Yes, sir."

"Both on the third and on the second?"

"Yes, sir."

"She had gone to the Lorenzo Hotel directly from the apartment in the Siglet Manor Apartments?"

"That is correct—yes, sir.''

"Leaving the Siglet Manor shortly after two o'clock?" Mason asked.

"Yes, sir. She left the apartment at eleven minutes past two, if you want the exact time.''

"Now did you *see* her drop anything in the garbage can?"

"No, sir. I've been very careful to state only what I actually saw. I was shadowing her, but I didn't want to be noticed, so I sort of kept behind her, out of sight. While she

172

had her back turned toward me, she picked up the lid of the garbage can; at that moment her body hid what her hands were doing. Then she *apparently* dropped something in. As soon as she started to turn, I ducked around a corner and got back to the lobby."

"And she returned to the lobby?"

"That's right."

"Where you kept her under observation until approximately what time?"

"Well, she didn't stay in the hotel lobby. The two women were there for a while and did some telephoning. Then they went out and did some shopping."

"It certainly seems to me, Your Honor, that all this is far afield," Gulling said.

"I think so too," Judge Lindale ruled. "It may be very interesting to the defendant, and it might constitute a great temptation for a fishing expedition, but it would hardly seem proper cross-examination."

"I'm sorry, Your Honor," Mason said. "I'll ask no more questions of the witness."

"Anything about the matter on which he was examined on direct examination is perfectly permissible," Judge Lindale said.

"No, Your Honor, I feel I have covered the ground and I have no desire to appear to be taking advantage of the Court's request that we expedite the examination."

"Any redirect?"

"I certainly have, Your Honor," Gulling said. "Now then, Mr. Folsom, you have been asked whether or not you saw the defendant drop anything in that garbage can. I want to ask you just one question. If she *had* dropped anything, could you have seen what it was?"

"No, sir, I tried to explain that. From the position in which I stood, I could not see what her right hand was doing; her body screened the motion. In fact, I didn't see her left *hand* at all. But I did see her bend over the garbage can, and I saw her left arm come up and the top of the can come up with it. I then saw her replace the cover on the can."

"That is all," Gulling said.

"Just a moment. In view of this last redirect," Mason said, "I have a few more questions of the witness. Mr. Folsom, you couldn't see either one of the defendant's hands?"

"I've said so several times."

"I just wanted to have it clear in the record. But you did see her left arm come up, raising the lid of the garbage can?"

"Yes, sir."

"From which you assumed that her left hand was holding the handle of the lid?"

"Naturally."

"Now then, did you see her right arm move?"

"I've tried to explain that her body screened whatever her right hand was doing."

"I'm not talking about her hand—I'm talking about her arm. Did you see her *arm* move?"

"No, sir."

"Her right shoulder move?"

"Well, now, wait a minute, Mr. Mason. I am not entirely sure, but—thinking back to it—I believe there *was* some slight motion of the elbow and shoulder, the sort one would make in gently tossing some object into a receptacle."

"You were transmitting reports to the Interstate Investigators?"

"Yes, sir."

"And were under instructions to telephone a report in every half-hour?"

"If we were where we could conveniently get to a phone, yes."

"How many men were on the job?"

"Two."

"You were shadowing Adelle Winters, and another person was shadowing Eva Martell?"

"Right."

"Now at the time you saw the defendant Winters do this," Mason said, "or within a very few minutes afterwards, you telephoned a report to the Interstate Investigators, didn't you?"

"Yes, sir."

"And in that report you stated that she had raised the lid of the garbage pail and *looked into* the garbage can."

"I believe so. That's right, yes."

"Now, as a part of *looking into* it, wouldn't she have had to move her right elbow or right shoulder?"

"Certainly not."

"And at the time you made that report, you had no idea she had *dropped something into* the garbage can?"

"I wouldn't go so far as to say that I 'had no idea' of it."

"But all your report stated was that she had *looked into* the can?"

"Yes."

"Which was all you thought she was doing, at the time."

"Well, it was one interpretation of what she had done."

"And you so reported to your agency?"

"Yes."

"Your recollection *then* of what she had done was fresher than it is now, wasn't it?"

"I don't think so—I think I recollect it just as well now as I did when I made the report."

"But your original impression was that she was only *looking into* the garbage can?"

"Well, if you want to put it that way—yes."

"At the time you made your report, the recollection was quite fresh in your mind. Now, about how long was it, after she went to the garbage can, that you telephoned your report?"

"I telephoned two or three minutes afterward. When I returned to the lobby, my associate took over and kept both parties under observation while I telephoned."

"And within two or three minutes after the garbage-can episode, the two defendants were together in the lobby?"

"That's right."

"And in your report to the agency you said that she had *looked into* the garbage can."

"Yes, sir."

"You hadn't had that garbage can under observation earlier?"

"No, sir."

"And didn't have any occasion to have it under observation afterward?"

"No, sir."

"Therefore you don't know but that this defendant merely did *look into* the garbage can and didn't *put anything into* it?"

"Well, I guess so, if you want to get technical," Folsom replied.

"I don't want to get unduly technical, but the point may prove to be rather important in this case."

"Well, if you want my frank opinion," Folsom said, "at that time I may have said she only *looked* inside, but the way I feel about it now is that I'm absolutely certain she lifted the lid of the garbage can and *dropped* something inside."

"Why didn't that interpretation occur to you at the time you telephoned your report?"

"I can't say," Folsom answered. "Probably I didn't consider the distinction particularly significant then."

"That's exactly the point I am trying to establish," said Mason. "What has colored your recollection now is the realization that the point *is* significant."

"I don't agree that it has 'colored my recollection' at all! It has just made me think back a little more carefully. I'm absolutely positive now that she *dropped* something into that garbage can."

"Just as positive as you were at twenty-three minutes past

two on the third day of this month that she had merely *looked into* it?"

"That's a rather harsh way of putting it, Mr. Mason."

"And *that's* a rather poor way of answering the question."

"I . . . she dropped something into that can."

"You're sure she did—now?"

"Yes."

"You weren't sure on the third?"

"Well—no—if you're going to split hairs!"

"That's all," Mason said.

"No redirect," Gulling said.

"Your next witness, Counselor."

"At this point I wish to recall Sam Dixon for a question," Gulling said.

"Very well."

The judge said to Dixon, "You have already been sworn. Go ahead and answer the questions."

"Mr. Dixon," Gulling asked, "did you have occasion on the afteroon of the third to visit the Lorenzo Hotel and inspect a garbage can there?"

"I did."

"What did you do?"

"I raised the cover of the garbage can, being careful not to leave any fingerprints on it. I found the can about two-thirds full of garbage. I emptied the garbage out on a piece of canvas, and in that garbage I found a Colt .32-caliber revolver, number 14581."

"And what did you do with the revolver?"

"Taking great care not to leave any fingerprints on it, and not to smudge any fingerprints that might already be on it— in spite of the fact that it had been right in the middle of wet garbage . . ."

"Never mind explaining why there were no fingerprints on the gun—just answer the question. What did you do?"

"I delivered the gun to Alfred Korbel."

"Mr. Korbel is the expert on ballistics and fingerprinting for the Police Department?"

"He is."

"And when did you deliver the weapon to him?"

"Both the weapon and the garbage-can lid were delivered at approximately seven forty-five on the evening of that day."

"The third of this month?"

"Yes, sir."

"You may inquire."

"No questions," Mason said.

"Court will take a recess for ten minutes," Judge Lindale ruled.

Mason caught Paul Drake's eye.

Paul nodded.

18

Ten minutes later, when Court was reconvened, Gulling said, "My next witness will be Alfred Korbel."

Taking the witness stand, Alfred Korbel qualified himself as an expert in ballistics and fingerprints.

"I show you a certain revolver, being a Colt .32-caliber, number 14581, and ask if you have ever seen it before?"

"I have—yes, sir."

"When?"

"I first saw it at about seven forty-five in the evening of the third of this month when it was delivered to me by Sam Dixon. I made several tests with it in my laboratory, and saw it again at approximately midnight—the night when the defendant Adelle Winters identified it as being a gun that belonged to her."

"You have made tests with this gun?"

"I have—yes, sir."

"Did you examine it for fingerprints?"

"Yes, sir."

"Did you find any?"

"No."

"Can you explain why there were none?"

"When the gun was delivered to me, it was covered with a coating of slime. There were bits of garbage adhering to portions of the gun as well as to an empty cartridge case that was in one cylinder. There were also bits of garbage in the barrel. Considering that the gun had been packed in garbage which had subsequently been stirred up, I should hardly expect to find any legible prints on it. Now, that sounds rather complicated," Korbel said with an apologetic smile;

"but what I'm trying to say is that if the gun—as the evidence indicates and as I understand is the case—was packed for some hours in a garbage can, to which more garbage was added from time to time, I should hardly expect to find fingerprints on it."

"What was the condition of the gun—that is, as to being loaded?"

"Five chambers were loaded, and one had been recently fired. This one contained an empty cartridge case."

"Did you make tests with the bullet handed you by the autopsy surgeon some time on the evening of the third?"

"I did—yes, sir."

"And without at this time asking you to tell where that bullet came from, I will ask you what your tests showed."

"They showed that the bullet had been fired from that gun."

"And you made tests of the handle on the lid of the garbage pail for fingerprints?"

"I did, yes."

"What did you find?"

"May I have that brief case, please?" Korbel asked.

Gulling handed it to him.

Korbel opened it and took out a set of photographs. "This photograph, taken with the aid of a mirror," he said, "shows the under side of the garbage can's handle. The handle shows several latents—some of them smudged, some clearly indentifiable."

"Directing your attention to the latent enclosed in a circle," Gulling said, "did you identify that latent print?"

"I did. That is the print of the middle finger of the left hand of the defendant, Adelle Winters."

"You may inquire," Gulling snapped.

"There are several latent prints on that handle?" Mason asked.

"That's right. They're quite plain, Mr. Mason."

"You can make out several of them plainly enough to identify them?"

"You mean to compare them with other prints?"

"Yes."

"That's right."

"You are employed by the police? That is, you are connected with the city police?"

"As an expert, yes."

"And you take orders from the police?"

"I don't understand just how you mean that. If you wish to imply that the police tell me what to say, you are wrong."

"But they tell you what to do?"

"Well . . . yes."

"So that when the police are working up a case against a person, you are biased insofar as that person is concerned?"

"How do you mean?"

"Take the instant case," Mason said. "You were and are trying to get evidence connecting Adelle Winters with the murder. You aren't *investigating* the murder, but just trying to implicate Mrs. Winters."

"I don't see where there's any difference. It's all the same thing."

"No it isn't. Take these fingerprints for instance. The minute you identified one of these prints as that of Adelle Winters that was all you wanted, wasn't it?"

"Naturally."

"In other words, you were interested in the latents on the garbage pail only to the extent of trying to prove a case against her?"

"Well, I guess so, yes; but I don't see what you're trying to establish, Mr. Mason. Naturally, if she had handled the lid of the garbage pail, that was evidence. I was trying to establish that."

"Exactly, and you didn't try to find out to whom those other latents belonged?"

The witness smiled. "Oh that! Dozens of persons had access to that garbage pail. It was a public place, so to speak. Many people from the kitchen of the café had access to the garbage pail and had lifted it during the afternoon. I am willing to admit that I was concerned only with finding and identifying a print proving that the defendant Adelle Winters had at some time previous to my examination lifted the cover."

"Exactly!" Mason said. "In other words, you wanted to find one thing in order to establish a case against this defendant. When you found it, you quit looking for anything else. Isn't that right?"

"In that particular place, yes."

"Why didn't you try to identify those other prints?"

"Because I wasn't concerned with them. I was instructed only to find out whether the garbage can had been handled by the defendant Winters."

"And when you said you assumed that the cover had been lifted several times during the afternoon—because further garbage had been deposited—you didn't have any ground for that assumption, did you?"

"Well . . . yes, I did."

"Such as what?"

"Well . . . of course, it's obvious that it *must* have been done."

"What is there in the evidence that makes you think so?"

"Well . . . nothing that I personally have seen. But it's obvious from the evidence."

"Just point out the part of the evidence that makes it obvious that additional garbage got put in subsequently."

"Why," Korbel said, "take Sam Dixon's evidence. When he found the gun it was pretty well down inside the garbage—which shows that more garbage had been piled on top of the gun after it had been thrown in."

"How does it show that?"

"Come, come!" Gulling interposed. "This is merely wrangling with a witness about an interpretation of evidence. It's up to the Court to make that interpretation."

"Quite right," Mason said. "I am just trying to establish the bias of this witness, Your Honor. Here is a man who has admitted that he examined the evidence only for the purpose of building up a case against the defendant Winters—not for the purpose of trying to find out what had actually happened."

"But isn't it obvious that exactly that *must* have happened?" Judge Lindale asked, a little impatiently.

"It is not, Your Honor."

Lindale's face showed surprise. "I'd be glad to hear Counsel on that," he said skeptically.

"The assumption is," said Mason, "that—because this gun was found, shall we say, *buried* in the garbage—from time to time during the afternoon additional garbage had been dumped in. Now, if the Court please, bear in mind the time element. Because of the shortage of help, the dining room at the Lorenzo Hotel closes at one forty-five in the afternoon and does not open again until six-thirty. I believe that a check-up among the kitchen help will reveal that the last lot of garbage during daylight hours is deposited shortly before two in the afternoon, and that no further lots are put in till seven-fifty in the evening.

"Now, if the Court will bear with me for a moment and look at the evidence, the Court will notice rather a peculiar situation. *If* the defendant Winters tossed a gun into the garbage can at two-twenty in the afternoon, and *if* more garbage did get piled on top of that gun before the time when the police turned out the contents on a canvas, *then* there would have been a good case of circumstantial evidence. But if *no* garbage was put in between the time the defendant was seen there and the time the police spilled out the contents, *then* it is obvious that—whatever the defendant Winters did—she certainly did not put the gun there. It must have been put there some minutes *earlier*, before she went out."

"How's that?" Judge Lindale asked in a puzzled tone.

"The testimony of the prosecution's own witness, Thomas Folsom, indicates that the defendant Winters was more likely to have been merely *looking into* the garbage can than to have been *putting something into it*."

"That's merely the strained interpretation you put on this testimony," Gulling snapped irritably.

"Obviously," Mason said, "it may have been possible for the witness to drop a gun into the garbage can; but she certainly couldn't have *pushed* it down deep into the garbage—for, if she had, her right hand would have been smeared with garbage and she would have had to go and wash it off. Indeed, in order to push the gun deep she would have had to roll up her sleeve—and she certainly didn't do that, or the witness Folsom would have seen the motions she made."

"He couldn't see her hands," Gulling said.

"He couldn't see her hands, but he could see her shoulder and her elbow. Had she pushed anything deep into the garbage, the witness Folsom certainly would have seen her do it."

"Yes," Judge Lindale said, "one would conclude as much, from the witness's description of what he saw. Of course, Mr. Mason, you didn't ask him specifically whether the motions he did see were consistent with a thrust deep into the garbage?"

"Certainly not," Mason said. "He was the prosecution's witness. Had I given him that idea, he would have changed his recollection again! The fact remains that his own statement made shortly after two-twenty on the third is far more eloquent than anything he's said since then. At that time he thought the defendant had merely *looked inside* the garbage can. It had only been since that day that he has built up a purely synthetic recollection of seeing the defendant 'toss' something into the garbage can. If it were now suggested to him that she really must have been 'thrusting' something deep into the garbage, he would stretch his recollection accordingly, and would soon have convinced himself that he had seen her 'thrust' something deep into the garbage!"

"A most interesting point," Judge Lindale said. "Has the prosecution any suggestion or explanation?"

"The prosecution has not," Gulling said angrily. "The defendant Winters is plainly guilty of cold-blooded, deliberate murder. Only a fraction of the evidence is in at the present time. Our next witness will show that the motive of the crime was robbery; that the defendant Winters had concealed on her person a wallet containing slightly more than three thousand dollars which had been taken from the body of Robert Hines."

"Or picked up somewhere by the defendant," Mason put in.

"That will be your contention, of course," Gulling sneered. "You'll claim that she was walking along the street and what should she happen on but a wallet? She picked it up and meant to look inside, but it was dark, and—"

"Come, come," Judge Lindale said. "There's no occasion for sarcasm, Counselor; the evidence in regard to the wallet will stand or fall by itself. But right now Mr. Mason has just made an interesting suggestion about the position of the weapon. Now, as I understand it, Counselor, you cannot prove that the weapon was on top of the garbage?"

"How should I know?" Gulling retorted sullenly. "When the police turned the garbage can over, they naturally mixed the contents all up."

"But," said Judge Lindale, "the witness Dixon lifted the lid off—must have, in order to take the gun out. If he had seen the gun there on top of the garbage he would have picked it up and *not* ordered the garbage all dumped out."

"Exactly," Mason resumed. "That, of course, is why I examined the witness in the way I did."

"Have you," the judge asked him, "checked on the matter of when further lots of garbage are deposited?"

"We have, Your Honor. Our information is that on that day no additional lots were deposited from two in the afternoon until seven-fifty at night."

"Has the prosecution made any such check?" Judge Lindale asked.

"The prosecution has not," Gulling said, with increasing

irritation. "The prosecution has enough evidence right now to convict both of these defendants in front of a jury, let alone have them bound over."

"I understand," Judge Lindale said, "and the eventual disposition of the case may be quite another matter. But the Court calls to the attention of Counsel that this is a case involving a charge of first-degree murder. If there is any legitimate conflict in the evidence, it would seem that the prosecution ought to be as anxious to investigate as the defense is. It appears to this Court obvious that, considering the evidence as it now stands, the defendant Winters could not have thrust the weapon down deep into that garbage can. I assume that it has been identified as the murder weapon?"

"It has, Your Honor."

"Then I suggest that we continue this case until tomorrow morning," Judge Lindale said; "and that the prosecution, with the aid of the police, give special attention to ascertaining the facts about that garbage can and whether more garbage was added between two-twenty in the afternoon and the time when the gun was discovered. Court is adjourned."

Harry Gulling pushed back his chair and rose from the table usually occupied by the prosecution counsel. His manner was grim and determined as he marched across to the defense table.

"Mr. Mason," he said crisply.

Mason got up and turned to face him.

"I had hoped that before evening the case would have been sufficiently presented so that all the facts would be before the Court and the public, and the defendants bound over."

Mason merely nodded, watching the man in curious appraisal.

"Unfortunately," Gulling went on, "owing to your tactics the situation has changed. You have confused the issues as well as the Court, and this has to some extent changed my own plans."

Mason still said nothing.

"Only to *some* extent, however."

Out of the corner of his eye Mason saw two newspaper photographers holding their cameras in readiness.

"I feel," Gulling went on, "that it is only fair to tell you now that my basic strategy has not been changed. I hand you herewith, Mr. Perry Mason, a subpoena to appear before the Grand Jury of this county at the hour of seven this evening." And he pushed a paper at Mason.

Simultaneously the synchronized flashbulbs of two cameras flared into brilliance as photographers recorded the serving of the subpoena.

"Thank you," Mason said, and calmly pocketed it.

"And I warn you, Mason," Gulling went on, as the photographers hurried away to get their pictures developed in time to make the afternoon editions, "you're going to be faced with a charge of perjury on the one hand or of being an accessory on the other. I now have evidence indicating that you picked up Eva Martell at the streetcar on the evening of the murder and spirited her away. I think that a certain party who runs a rooming house, and who has apparently been trying to protect you, is guilty of perjury. Investigation now discloses that she is a former client of yours whom you successfully defended some time ago. I feel it is only fair to tell you this much, so that you will be prepared."

Mason advanced a step. "All right," he said, his face granite-hard, "you've prepared me. Now *I'll* prepare *you*. You've made a personal issue out of this. You've walked into court on this case personally. I assume you'll be with the Grand Jury tonight to examine me personally. You have a political job. I haven't. You can turn the heat on me, and I can take it. If I turn the heat on you, I don't think you can take it."

"Right now," Gulling said, "I am the one who is in the position to turn on the heat, and it's going to be very hot, Mr. Mason!"

19

Mason, pacing back and forth across the floor of his office, said to Paul Drake, "The thing that bothers me in this case, Paul, is Mae Bagley."

"What about her?"

"She tried to protect me. They came down on her like a ton of bricks without giving her any warning. As soon as that taxi driver told where he had picked Eva Martell up, the cops dashed down and grabbed Mae Bagley."

"And she told them she'd never seen Eva Martell before?"

"That's right."

"Was she under oath?" Drake asked.

"Not then she wasn't. Shortly afterward they dragged her up before the Grand Jury, and she was under oath then, of course. They'll probably examine her again tonight."

"Shucks, Perry, no matter how crude her first story was, have her stick to it. Of course, she can simply refuse to answer on the ground that doing so might incriminate her."

"It isn't that simple," Mason said. "Gulling is the type of technical-minded chap with a very exalted opinion of himself and an exaggerated idea of his own importance. He's shrewd enough to know all the technical angles, and he's getting ready to throw the book at everyone."

"Well, they've evidently got the deadwood on you now, Perry. They know that you took Eva Martell to that rooming house. Can't you show that Gulling gave you until noon to produce her; that you told her to surrender herself to the police well within the time limit given you by Gulling—and let it be your word and hers against what is merely Gulling's insinuation that she *wasn't* on the way to surrender herself when she was arrested? It seems to me you could beat the case that way, hands down."

"That isn't the point," Mason said. "Mae Bagley tried to protect me. She said that she hadn't had Eva Martell in her house. Now then, the minute she changes her story they get her on two counts. First, for failing to keep an accurate register of the people in her rooming house, and second, because of her previous false statement. They also make her an accessory after the fact in hiding a person accused of murder. And if I try to protect myself by telling what did happen, I've put Mae Bagley in a spot. The minute I open up, I've hooked that Bagley woman on all sorts of charges."

"Oh, oh!" Drake said.

"And when I get in front of the Grand Jury, I've got to try to talk my way out or else take a beating."

"Can't you claim professional privilege?"

"Only as to what my client may have said to me. And there's that twelve o'clock surrender deadline. . . ."

"Can't you show that that's just an absurd technicality?"

Mason grinned. "I've been throwing technicalities at the district attorney's office for a long time now, and I'd put myself in a pretty poor light if I started yelling that I was being crucified on a technicality!"

"Yes, I suppose so," Drake admitted. "What's the idea of planting the purse so Gulling would find it, Perry?"

Mason grinned. "I'm letting Gulling interpret the law, Paul."

"What law?"

"The portion of the law which defines what is a reasonable time. I may not have to use it, but knowing him as I do, I realize he'll try to hook me on some trival offense in case I should wriggle off the hook on this other charge. . . . However, he's got all of us pretty well hooked on that other stuff, what with all the evidence he's turned up.

"Of course," Mason went on, "the situation would be

simplified if it weren't for that wallet. Because the gun testimony is considerably mixed up by this time."

"Didn't Adelle Winters throw the gun into that garbage can?"

"I'm beginning to think she didn't."

"Then what's the explanation?"

"She is lying about the gun. She didn't have it, and it never was up there on the sideboard, and she didn't take it with her. But she knew who *did* have it, and that person had agreed to plant the gun in the garbage can. According to my idea right now, Adelle Winters merely looked inside to see whether it was there."

"That sounds rather complicated, Perry."

Mason suddenly turned to Della Street. "Get the Lorenzo Hotel for me, Della. I want to talk with somebody who knows about the records that have been kept there."

"What are you getting at, Perry?" Drake asked as Della Street put through the call. "Do you think that Adelle Winters had some accomplice at the hotel?"

"One thing in the case has never been explained," said Mason. "It's simple, obvious, and significant—and therefore everyone has completely overlooked it."

"What's that?"

"How did it happen that Adelle Winters and Eva Martell went to the Lorenzo Hotel in the first place?" Mason asked.

"Well, they wanted to go to some public place. They didn't want to go home, and . . ."

"There are lots of hotels," Mason said. "Why pick the Lorenzo in particular?"

"Well, they *had* to pick one of them."

"But what made them hit on that one? I—"

"They're on the line," Della Street told him.

Mason picked up the telephone and said, "This is Perry Mason, the lawyer. I want to find out something about a former guest of the hotel."

"Yes, Mr. Mason, we'll be glad to give you any assistance we can."

"I want you please to look back through your records and let me know whether an Adelle Winters ever had a room there."

"I can tell you right now, Mr. Mason. I saw her name in the papers, and of course there's the fact that the police found a weapon here. Perhaps you didn't know it, but at one time she worked as a waitress in the dining room here. It's called the Lorenzo Café. It's operated under separate management, though in connection with the hotel."

"How long ago?" Mason asked.

"A little over a year ago."

"How long was she there?"

"Three months."

"Does anyone else know about this?"

"Yes, sir, the district attorney's office knows it."

"How do you know?"

"Because they asked me and I told them."

"When?"

"Day before yesterday."

"Thank you," Mason said. "Have they subpoenaed you as a witness?"

"Not me, but the proprietor of the café. Would you like to talk with him?"

"Definitely not," Mason said. "Thanks for the information. Good-by."

As he hung up he met Paul Drake's dismayed eyes.

"Well, there you are," Mason said. "That's that! I know now why the two women went to the Lorenzo Hotel, and also how Mrs. Winters knew where the garbage pails were kept. She worked there for three months about a year ago!"

"She *did*?" Drake exclaimed. "I see. But what about the gun?"

"According to Folsom, she raised the cover and *looked inside*. Now then, the gun was found under quite a layer of garbage. Suppose she is lying all along the line? Suppose, as I suggested a few minutes ago, she *didn't* leave the gun behind on the apartment sideboard? Suppose someone else

191

had the gun? Suppose this person phoned her and said that he or she had killed Hines and tossed the gun into that garbage can? Now, who could have killed Hines and then been able to count on the coöperation of Adelle Winters?"

"Eva Martell," Drake replied promptly.

Mason paused to give that consideration. "You may have something there, Paul. But I'd be more inclined to say it was— Just when was the noontime garbage put in there, Paul?"

"We've checked up on that for you. It was at two-ten that the kitchen man came out with a big tubful of garbage, which he dumped into the middle garbage can. The police have been checking up on him—trying to get him to say he might be mistaken about the hour, that it might have been some time after two-twenty. But the man insists that it was exactly ten minutes past two; he's sure, because he kept looking at the clock—he had a date at three and he was trying to get cleaned up and out of there and change his clothes in time to keep that date. And here's a strange thing: he can't swear to it, but he *thinks* the pail was about two-thirds full of garbage when he finished dumping his tubful.

"Get what that means, Perry? The gun must have been in there *before* two-ten, and the last lot of garbage put in must have covered it up. The man was in a hurry, so he just raised the lid and dumped the stuff in. And five or ten minutes later, when Adelle Winters looked inside, the gun wasn't visible because it was covered over."

Mason exclaimed, "Paul, *if* we can show that the gun was actually in the garbage pail at two-ten, we've got an alibi! Because Adelle Winters didn't reach the hotel until two-fifteen. How about the time of death? What did you learn about that?"

"Autopsy surgeon says some time between one o'clock and three o'clock in the afternoon. Can't get any closer than that."

"Well," Mason went on, "Eva Martell was in that apartment until five minutes of two. They went out of the apartment house at eleven minutes past. Which gives a period of sixteen minutes between their leaving the apartment itself and their departure from the building."

By this time Drake was excited too. "Let's look at it now from the other angle. Who do we know of who could have walked into that apartment naturally—gone in quietly without rousing comment? In the first place, Helen Reedley; she has a key to the apartment. Next, Carlotta Tipton; she could have tapped on the door and Hines would have let her in. Then, of course, there was the maid . . ."

"And," Mason said, "I'm inclined to add Arthur Clovis to that list. I imagine that he had a key to the apartment, and that that's one of the things that get him all churned up whenever the subject is mentioned. I don't suppose there's any way of finding out for sure, is there, Paul?"

"Not unless we could think up some way of frisking him, and that would be dangerous. Anyhow, if he ever had a key he's probably ditched it by now," Paul Drake added.

"Well," Mason went on, "how about Helen Reedley? We don't know where she was, around the time the murder was committed. She *says* she was looking for Hines in the restaurant, that she missed him there and tried telephoning. Suppose she talked with Carlotta, and suppose Carlotta told her that Hines was up in the other apartment? . . . No, Carlotta's not likely to have done that . . . But when you come right down to it, Paul, there are a lot of people who can't account for their time between say one forty-five and two-fifteen."

Drake nodded.

"Not that that simplifies my problem much." Mason sounded grim. "The police are going to get after me in the matter of concealing Eva Martell after I knew she was perhaps implicated in the murder. And they'll get after Mae Bagley for making a false statement, for failing to keep a register, *and* for being an accessory. . . . Tell you what you do, Paul. Get a likely looking operative to put on some bib overalls, take a satchel, go around to various apartments in the building where Arthur Clovis lives, knock on the doors and announce loudly that he's in the key-manufacturing business and that he's trying to get old keys for use as blanks. Have him say he'll pay five cents apiece for old keys."

"But you *can't make* a new key from an old one, Perry— you know that yourself!"

"That's just the point," Mason said. "Clovis is the dreamy type. He hasn't very much executive ability. Put yourself in his shoes. Someone who looks like a key man comes to the door and says he's collecting old keys. He has a satchel open that is half full of keys. He offers five cents apiece. Now suppose Clovis has a key that is burning a hole in his pocket. Here's a chance to get rid of it. He isn't going to stop to question the other chap's statement. He'll toss the key into the satchel, take his nickel, and think he's done a good job!"

"What *will* the fellow have in the satchel?" Drake asked. "I can't scare up that many keys . . ."

"Get some iron washers," Mason told him; "something the fellow can rattle around inside it."

"Okay, Perry, I'll try it. It *may* work."

"You'll have to get busy," Mason said, looking at his watch. "Time is running out damn fast."

"I can make a stab at it within an hour by using the telephone, and—"

"And that's twice too long," Mason interrupted. "Have a man with a satchel up there inside of thirty minutes."

Drake groaned. "If I'd said thirty minutes in the first place, you'd have cut it to fifteen. Let me get out of here, Della, and get to work before he thinks of something else."

Drake had lost his drawl. His long legs moved in swift strides as he crossed the office and jerked the door open.

When he had gone, Mason looked at his watch, then glanced across at Della Street. "No need to wait, Della."

"I'll stay on the job," she said. "You may get an idea."

"Wish I *could* get one! Hang it, Della—there's something in the case, some central point that's eluding me." He resumed his pacing of the floor.

"How about calls, Chief?" Della asked. "I hear the telephone in the other office buzzing."

"Let's see who it is," Mason said. "If it's a client, tell him I'm not in."

Della Street went out to the switchboard and returned in a moment to say, "It's Cora Felton. She says she has to talk with you, that it's very important. I've put her on this line."

Mason picked up the receiver on his desk telephone. "Hello, Cora. What is it?"

"Mr. Mason, I'm so sorry. I—"

"That's all right, I was up here working on the case anyway."

"No, no—I mean so sorry about what's happened."

"What?"

"I'm afraid I didn't do the right thing in getting you to represent Aunt Adelle. I did tell you that she isn't always reliable in what she says, but I didn't realize how far she would—"

"Come on," Mason interrupted. "Out with it, Cora! Never mind the alibis or apologies. What is it?"

"Oh, Mr. Mason, I . . . I hardly know how to tell you."

"Just *tell* it!"

"Well, I have just been visiting with Aunt Adelle. I had a pass to get in and see her . . . Well, she told me that what she had said wasn't entirely the truth."

"About what?"

"About the wallet."

Mason groaned. "Do you mean to say she *did* get it from the man's dead body?"

"I . . . I don't know, Mr. Mason."

"Exactly what did she tell you?"

"Well, she *said* she got it afterwards; that most of the things happened just as she told you, but that the wallet was there after she came back to the apartment. I was talking with her about how fine you had been and how marvelously you were handling the case. Well, then she started to cry, and she said she felt like a heel!"

"Where are you now?" Mason asked.

"In a drugstore about two blocks from the City Hall."

"Hop a taxi and get up here," Mason said. "You'll just have time to make it if you hurry. I must see you before I go to the Grand Jury room."

When he hung up he said to Della Street, "Here's a pretty how-do-you-do! Did you listen in?"

"Yes, and I took notes in shorthand."

"Good girl! I— Oh, Lord, there's somebody at the door."

Insistent knuckles were pounding on the exit door of Mason's private office. Mason nodded to Della, who went and opened the door. It was Mae Bagley.

"Oh, Mr. Mason," she bagan impetuously, "I wouldn't do this for worlds! Only—well, I've been subpoenaed to appear before the Grand Jury again, and Mr. Gulling has been talking to me—"

"Sit down," Mason told her. "What did Mr. Gulling say?"

"He said they had all the evidence they really needed to show that you had put Eva Martell in my rooming house, but they wanted to really clinch the case; that I would get complete immunity if I'd tell them the truth; that they wouldn't bother me about my license or about being an accessory. They'd take it for granted that you had influenced me. He said that everything would be all right—there'd be no perjury charge, or anything."

"What did you say?" Mason said.

"I looked him in the eyes and said, 'Why, Mr. Gulling, I can't understand how you could possibly make such a proposition. I should think you'd realize that a woman in my position couldn't afford to lie. If I had ever seen Eva Martell before, or if Mr. Mason had brought her to my house, I'd have told you!"

"Make it stick?"

"I don't know . . ."

Mason said, "Look, Mae, my advice to you is to take advantage of that offer and tell the truth."

"Do you mean that?"

"Of course I mean it."

"You mean to come right out and tell them *everything* that happened?"

"Yes—come right out and tell them everything that happened," Mason repeated. "You shouldn't have lied to protect me in the first place. You've got yourself in bad, and I certainly don't want to hide behind your skirts."

"Why—why, I had no idea of telling them! I just thought you ought to know."

"You're on your way up there now?" Mason asked.

"Yes."

"Go tell them the whole story," Mason said, "and say that I told you to."

"Well . . . well, thanks, Mr. Mason. I . . . gosh, I had no idea you'd tell me anything like that."

"That's my advice to you," Mason said, "and be on your way."

"Thank you, Mr. Mason. I just want you to know how I feel . . . I'd do anything for you, anything on earth, even go to jail!"

"That's fine," Mason told her with a smile, "but you just tell them the truth and things will straighten out all right."

"Thank you, Mr. Mason. I . . . I'll see you up there, I suppose."

"Probably," Mason said.

She walked over to the exit door, nodded to Della Street, gave Mason a warm smile, and before the automatic door check had pulled the door into place, they could hear the clack of her heels along the corridor.

Mason looked across at Della Street and shrugged. "As an attorney, it was the only advice I could give—just to tell the truth."

Della Street nodded and got to her feet, saying, "My nose shines. You'll be here for a few minutes yet?"

"Yes, Cora Felton is coming up."

Della let herself out into the corridor and the door closed. Mason groaned, looked at his watch, and resumed his restless walking of the floor.

Della Street ran down the corridor to catch Mae Bagley at the elevator. "Mae," she said in a quick whisper, "you understand, don't you?"

"What?"

"That was the only advice Mr. Mason *could* give you. If he had told you not to say anything, or to tell a falsehood, it would have been a conspiracy to commit perjury if—well, if it should ever come out."

"Listen, sister, you don't need to worry about me," Mae assured her. "You tell Mr. Mason to just go ahead with what he has to do and quit worrying about anything I might say. Anything Gulling gets out of me he can put in his eye!"

The two women looked at each other for a moment, and suddenly Mae Bagley's arms were around Della. "You poor kid!" she said. "You're shivering. Is it that bad?"

"Gosh," Della admitted, "I don't know, but I *am* worried."

"It'll be okay! Skip on in and give him a pat on the back. Tell him what I've just told you."

Della Street shook her head. "I can't tell him in so many words," she said. "It's one of those things nobody can ever *talk* about. We just— Well, at a time like this, we just have to take each other on faith."

The elevator cage lighted up the shaft and then came to a stop. As the door slid open Mae Bagley walked in, turned, and waved to Della encouragingly.

Della was walking slowly back to the office when the second cage came to a stop. The door slid open and Cora Felton hurried out.

"Oh, hello!" Della Street said. "The boss is waiting in

here. We only have a minute." And she took Cora back through the door to Mason's private office.

Mason, still pacing the floor, looked up as they entered.

"Hello, Cora," he said. "Sit down. Tell me what it is."

"Mr. Mason, I just don't know. I've completely lost confidence in Aunt Adelle. I can't understand why she would do a thing like that."

"What does she say now?"

"Well, she says she picked up the wallet and then wondered why Mr. Hines had left it there. Then she walked into the other room and found the body, and her first thought was that now perhaps nobody would know the wallet was missing and she could keep what was in it. She didn't know how much that was, but she could see that the wallet was pretty well filled with money. When she had a chance to look at it—while Eva was telephoning you and then the police—she saw the big bills and made up her mind she just wouldn't give it up. She's always had to fight her way through the world, and the world hasn't given her a square deal. People have done all sorts of mean things to her, and—"

"Never mind the justification," Mason said. "Tell me the rest of it."

"Well, when the police nabbed her and asked her where and when she'd got this wallet, she was frightened and lied because she thought that the only thing to do was to claim she'd found it *before* Mr. Hines was murdered. She says that at that time she didn't know Hines had been killed with her gun. That meant that the murder must have been committed while she was downstairs; she thought then that it had happened some time later—after she'd left the apartment."

Mason asked, "Any particular reason why she should have told you all that?"

"Yes, there was. The police had someone in a cell with her, a cellmate thrown in on a charge of murdering her husband. The woman was sweet and sympathetic, and she and Adelle started exchanging confidences. She told Aunt Adelle all about *her* case, and Aunt Adelle loosened up and told her quite a bit. Well, when Aunt Adelle was being taken out of the cell to go through some formality, one of the other prisoners waited until the matron had moved off a little way, and then she whispered some underworld jargon to Aunt Adelle—about buttoning her lips because they'd thrown a 'stoolie' in with her. For a moment it didn't register, and then Aunt Adelle got what it was all about, and now she's panic-stricken."

"She ought to be," Mason said grimly. "What a sweet mess *this* is!"

Della had been watching the time, and now she said, "You'll have to be leaving, Chief."

Mason nodded, picked up his brief case and hat.

"Does this make much difference, Mr. Mason?" Cora asked nervously.

"Does it make much difference!" Mason's tone was rough with sarcasm. "It only kicks her case out of the window. Once she admits falsifying that last sworn statement she made—" He broke off as the phone rang.

Della Street scooped up the receiver. "Hello. Yes—wait a minute, Paul. He's just leaving."

Mason quickly took the receiver from Della and said, "Hello, Paul. Anything new?"

Drake's voice was excited. "Anything new! Listen, Perry. We've got it! The guy fell for it like a ton of bricks. My man had a grip full of washers, and—"

"Never mind that," Mason cut in. "Give me the answer quick."

"The bird rummaged around in the drawers and sold him fifteen keys, and one of them had stamped on it 'Siglet Manor Apartments.'"

"You haven't fitted it to Helen Reedley's apartment?"

"Not yet, Perry. Have a heart—gosh, my man just got it. But we're on our way down there now."

"Okay," Mason said. "That's a load off my mind. It

looks as though we were beginning to get somewhere. You can see what happened. He told Helen Reedley what Hines had said, and Helen Reedley recognized it at once as a blackmailing approach . . . Okay, Paul, I've got it now. It may be a way out. If anything turns up, call me in the anteroom of the Grand Jury—I'll arrange things so I can take phone calls there. I'll have Della come along to hand me messages in case I can't go to the phone. Keep working on it. So long. I'm on my way."

Mason hung up and nodded to Della.

As she gave him his hat and brief case she said demurely, "I happened to see Mae in the hall, Chief. She's nice, isn't she?"

Mason stopped and looked at his secretary with a steady scrutiny. She met his eyes, her own all wide-eyed innocence.

"I mean she's just a good kid," Della added.

Mason circled her with his arm and drew her to him. "So are you!"

20

Mason caught Mae Bagley just outside the Grand Jury anteroom. He nodded his head with a slight inclination toward a bend in the corridor and Mae Bagley followed him around the corner.

"Who's in there?" Mason asked.

"Just about everybody."

"Can you remember names?"

She smiled. "I got *all* the names—that's why I'm out here waiting for you. I thought you'd like to know before you went in."

"Good girl!"

She said, "There's a man by the name of Clovis who I think has to testify about some numbers on some bills. He's a banker."

"I know him."

"And Sam Dixon—You know him all right. And Tom Folsom, and the woman Carlotta Tipton, who I think is going to testify about some phone calls, and Helen Reedley and Orville Reedley. Those last two are staging a typical husband-and-wife act, sitting on opposite sides of the room and glaring across at each other."

"All right. Now let me tell you something. You must have confidence in me and get this straight and do exactly as I tell you."

"Anything in the world you say, Mr. Mason."

"Did Della Street stop you in the corridor and tell you to disregard what I had said about—"

"Della Street?"

"My secretary."

"Heavens, no, Mr. Mason! She must have gone down to the ladies' room—I heard someone come out of your door, but I didn't . . ."

"Look here," Mason said, "you're lying. You can't afford to lie to me."

"No matter who asks me," she said, "I'd swear, and will always swear, that Della Street never said a word to me."

"All right," Mason said. "We'll let that go. But if she did, don't pay any attention to what she said. Here's what I want you to do. I want you to go to Gulling and tell him that you've changed your mind; that you're going to tell the truth if you can get an agreement giving you complete immunity from perjury, from being an accessory, from everything—but that you want that agreement in writing, and you want it signed by him. Now go to him right away and get that."

"But what shall I tell him when I once get the agreement?"

"Then," Mason said, "tell him the absolute truth, every single bit of it. Do you understand? Don't hide anything except—well, of course, you don't need to tell him about any conversation you may have had in the corridor outside my office."

"Don't worry, Mr. Mason—I wouldn't admit *that* conversation if Saint Peter himself asked me about it."

"Good girl!" Mason said. "Now go and get Gulling. I'll come in a minute or two after you so that it won't look suspicious."

"Oh, I've been in and out, smoking and walking around. They've got me tabbed as the nervous type. That'll make it look all the more convincing when I go to Gulling. He'll think I'm cracking under the strain. You're sure it's all right? That you want me to do it, Mr. Mason?"

"Yes. Tell him everything—except this: you remember that I didn't make any suggestions to you about not having Eva Martell sign the register. I just told you I wanted her to have a room where—"

"Yes, I remember that. Not putting her on the register was my own idea."

"Okay," Mason said. "Tell it the way it happened, and good luck to you!"

A few moments later, when Mae Bagley had had time to enter the room, Mason sauntered in.

Mae Bagley was whispering something to Gulling, and a moment later Gulling whisked her out of the room. The witnesses were kept waiting in hostile silence for a matter of some ten minutes. Then Gulling, looking triumphant, marched through the anteroom to the Grand Jury room and returned almost immediately. "Mr. Perry Mason," he said.

Mason entered the Grand Jury room.

"Mr. Mason," Gulling said, "you are called as a witness. The Grand Jury is investigating certain matters in connection with the murder of Robert Hines and with developments arising therefrom. I consider it only fair to tell you that you may be indicted yourself as an accessory or an accomplice of certain crimes. You are, of course, aware of your legal rights. You don't have to answer any question that might incriminate you; on the other hand, any failure to answer a pertinent question will be considered a contempt."

Mason settled himself in the witness chair and smiled frostily at Gulling. "Go right ahead, Mr. Gulling. Turn on your heat."

"I'm not calling for any privileged communication between you and your clients, Mr. Mason, but I *am* asking specifically whether, after you had learned of the murder of Robert Hines, you did not conceal Eva Martell from the police. Whether you didn't meet her at the streetcar stop nearest her apartment, put her in your automobile, and take her to a rooming house conducted by Mae Bagley, who is a former client of yours?"

Mason crossed his legs and nodded. "Why, certainly."

"What!" Gulling shouted.

"Certainly I did," Mason said. "Except that your entire premise is incorrect. I wasn't hiding her from the police."

"Who were you hiding her from?"

"Newspaper reporters," Mason said promptly. "You know how it is. Those chaps have a way of ferreting people out and getting interviews from them."

"But you did go to Mae Bagley's rooming house with this young woman, and you did tell Mae Bagley you wanted her buried where no one could find her?"

"That's exactly right," Mason said.

"Where no one could find her?"

"Right."

"No one?"

"Right again."

"Don't you understand that includes the police, Mr. Mason?"

"The police had already finished with her." Mason smiled. "They'd taken her statement and let her go."

"But they wanted her again shortly afterward."

"Well," Mason said, "I naturally can't be expected to read the minds of the police. As I understand it, the charge the Grand Jury is investigating on this point relates to my intention. I am telling you what my intention was. If you want to make anything else out of it, you'll have to do some proving!"

"The next morning you knew she was wanted by the police because I told you so."

"You certainly did," Mason said. "You also told me that I had until twelve o'clock to get her here. I told her to be sure and be at police headquarters and surrender before twelve o'clock. That discharged my responsibility, Mr. Gulling."

"No, it didn't. You didn't *get* her here by twelve o'clock."

"Isn't that rather technical? A cruising radio car picked her up."

"In a taxicab—which she *said* she was using to go to police headquarters. But she couldn't prove it!"

"Come, come, Mr. Gulling," Mason said, smiling

affably. "You're confusing your cart and your horse. That's a matter for you to take up with Eva Martell. My only connection with it was that I *told* her to be up here by twelve o'clock. Even, however, if she had disregarded my advice and made a dash out of the state by airplane, I'd still be in the clear."

Gulling, recognizing the force of Mason's argument, said coldly, "We'll pass that for the moment. There's also the question of your being an accessory after the fact of the crime of murder."

"Oh, that," Mason said casually.

"Yes, *that!*" Gulling snapped.

"Of course if you want to talk about the murder, this is going to be rather long drawn out. The defendants in the murder case are being tried in a preliminary hearing before Judge Lindale. But, if you're really interested in finding out something about that murder, you might ask some questions of your witness Arthur Clovis out there."

"Clovis?" the foreman of the Grand Jury asked. "Isn't he to be questioned?"

Gulling replied, "Just on the question of the numbers on the bills, for the purpose of identification."

"You might," said Mason, "get Clovis to tell you how it happened that he had a key to the Siglet Manor apartment in his possession, and why he was so anxious to get rid of that key, and—"

A deputy sheriff entered the room and said to Gulling, "This message to Mr. Mason has to be delivered immediately."

Gulling's face flushed. "Don't interrupt these proceedings to give messages to the witness. You should know better than that."

"But they said this was—"

"I don't care what they said. The Grand Jury is interrogating Mr. Mason."

Seeing the slip of paper in the deputy's hand, Mason extended his own hand, said, "Since the interruption has

206

already been made, I'll take the message," and coolly clamped his fingers about the folded paper before Gulling could object.

Mason unfolded the paper. The message was in Della Street's handwriting.

Drake just phoned. It's all a mistake about the key. It *is* to a Siglet Manor apartment, but not to Helen Reedley's—it's to Carlotta Tipton's. Apparently Arthur Clovis used to live there in that apartment at the Siglet Manor. After he and Helen fell for each other, she thought it would be safer for him to live somewhere else, so he moved out and Carlotta Tipton moved in. Gosh, I'm sorry!—Della.

Mason crumpled the sheet and slipped it into his pocket.

"If you're *quite* ready to answer questions," Gulling said, "and can take enough of your valuable time to comply with the requirements of the law, Mr. Mason . . ."

"What do you want to know?" Mason asked.

"What were you going to say about Arthur Clovis?" the foreman asked.

"Just that he had a key to the Siglet Manor Apartments," Mason said. "He used to live there."

"Well, isn't it natural for him to have a key, if he failed to surrender it when he moved?"

"I just wanted you to know that he had a key to the apartment house in which the body was found."

"You don't claim he had anything to do with the murder?"

"Heavens, no! I just wanted you to know the facts."

"I don't see what that fact has to do with it," Gulling said. "You don't claim that it was a key to the apartment where the murdered man was found, do you?"

"No, no," Mason said. "Nothing like that. It's a key to an apartment now occupied by a Carlotta Tipton, I believe. You might check on that."

"We know all about her," Gulling said.

"Girl friend of the dead man," Mason commented, his tone still casual. "She was quite jealous. Followed him when he went down to meet his death."

"How's that?" the foreman asked.

Mason looked at Gulling in surprise. "I thought you'd told him about that."

"You claim that Carlotta Tipton followed Robert Hines to the apartment of Helen Reedley?"

"That's right."

"But she told me she was asleep all afternoon!"

"She told me different," Mason said, "and in the presence of witnesses."

"How many witnesses?"

"Three."

"Disinterested?"

"Two of them were in my employ."

"And the third?"

"Paul Drake."

"Your detective?"

"That's right."

"A likely story," Gulling sneered.

"You don't believe it?"

"No."

"The jury that tries my client will," Mason told him, smiling.

"That doesn't affect your connection with what happened," Gulling said angrily. "You may draw a red herring across the trail when you get before the trial jury, but you can't do it here."

"It's no red herring." Mason was sparring for time. "Why don't you ask her?"

"I think that might be a good idea, Mr. Gulling," the foreman said.

Gulling yielded, though with bad grace. "You will retire to the outer room, Mr. Mason, and—"

"Why not let him stay right here?" the foreman suggested. "I'd like to hear what this woman says when she's confronted with Mr. Mason."

"It's illegal," Gulling said. "Under the law only the consulting experts can be present."

The foreman urged impatiently, "I want Mason here. He's a witness."

"Not being examined."

"Then he's a consulting expert."

"I warn you it's illegal."

"Then we'll take a recess for a while and just have a sort of informal meeting. Bring her in."

"You can't make her swear to her testimony if you're in recess."

"Never mind that for the present. Get her in here."

"Bring her in," Gulling told the deputy, again yielding with bad grace.

When Carlotta Tipton entered she smiled at the grand jurors, sat down, and carefully arranged her legs so as to show just enough stocking to interest them.

"Mr. Mason says," Gulling began, "that you admitted to him that you had followed Robert Hines to the Reedley apartment where he was later found murdered. What about it?"

She turned to Mason in surprise. "Mr. Mason said *that*?"

"He did."

"Why, Mr. Mason, how *could* you say a thing like that? I told you particularly when you called there that I had been sleeping all the afternoon; that I knew Robert was acquainted with a Helen Somebody, or had some business transactions with her; but that I didn't have the least idea who she was. And you could have knocked me down with a feather when I found it was a woman who had an apartment in the same building."

"You made that statement to Mr. Mason?" Gulling asked.

"Yes, sir, I did."

"Did Mr. Mason have witnesses present?"

"Yes. A flock of people trooped in—people who were working for him. And he told me that he was representing some clients and had to get them out of a murder charge; that if I could help him he'd appreciate it. I told him there wasn't a thing that I could say or do that would help him. And then he said that if I would say I'd been jealous of Robert it would help, and I told him I couldn't say that, because I knew that this business with 'Helen'—whoever she was—was merely a matter of business. And he asked me if I couldn't change my testimony just a little bit."

"He asked you to *change* your testimony?" Gulling demanded.

"That's right," she said demurely.

"You want to ask this witness any questions, Mr. Mason?" the foreman asked Mason.

"Just a moment. Just a moment," Gulling protested. "That's irregular."

"I don't care whether it's irregular or not," the foreman said. "As far as I'm concerned, Perry Mason is a lawyer, and a good one. He might cut a corner by trying to keep a client out of circulation, but if he says this woman said certain things to him, *I* don't think he's lying. And if he's got three witnesses to back him up, I want to know more about it. It seems to me the district attorney's office should show a little more concern over the possibility that this witness, Carlotta Tipton, may be the one that's committing perjury."

"Nevertheless, Mr. Mason can't examine witnesses. It's irregular and it's illegal."

The foreman said angrily, "Well, *I* can ask questions, and Mr. Mason can talk to *me*. Tell me what questions to ask, Mr. Mason."

"Ask her what time she went to sleep."

Carlotta Tipton replied angrily, "I don't look at my watch every time I go to sleep. It was right after lunch."

"Took her clothes off and went to sleep while Robert

Hines was in the apartment?" Mason asked the foreman. "You might inquire about that."

"You can't throw mud at me," Carlotta exclaimed. "I was fully dressed until after Bob Hines left the apartment."

Mason caught the foreman's eye and tapped his watch significantly.

"What time was that?" the foreman asked.

"About five minutes of two."

"And when did you see Hines again?"

"I never saw him again."

"You might ask her how long she slept," Mason said.

"All afternoon," Carlotta Tipton snapped back at Mason.

"This is *highly* irregular!" Gulling protested helplessly.

Ignoring him, Mason went on. "You can easily prove that's a lie. Helen Reedley had the number of the telephone in Miss Tipton's apartment; Adelle Winters had the phone number of that apartment; and Eva Martell had the number. That apartment was where they were to call Mr. Hines. And that phone was ringing pretty steadily all afternoon—and was answered by Carlotta Tipton."

"Of course," Gulling sneered, "Eva Martell and Adelle Winters would swear to anything to save their necks."

"Try Helen Reedley," Mason invited.

There was silence.

Carlotta Tipton broke it to say nervously, "Well, I did wake up long enough to answer the phone once or twice, but I rolled right over and went back to sleep. I didn't leave that apartment from five minutes to two onward!"

Gulling said coldly, "This hearing is getting somewhat out of hand. It seems to me that we should conduct it—"

The foreman said, "I'm not going to let a lawyer be smeared. I don't know how the other members feel about it, but if Mason has committed any crime I'm going to indict him. If he hasn't I'm going to exonerate him. And before I do *anything* I'm going to make mighty certain that he isn't being framed!"

Several heads nodded assent.

"Perry Mason is representing two persons who are guilty of robbery and murder," Gulling said.

Mason said, "Why don't you let the murder case wait until it's been tried in court, Gulling?"

"Because I don't have to. But if this Grand Jury is interested, I can show——"

"Wait a minute!" Mason interrupted.

He was on his feet, his eyes level-lidded with concentration, looking over the heads of the grand jurors, staring into space.

"Well?" the foreman asked after a moment.

Mason said abruptly, "I have a suggestion to make to this Grand Jury."

"What is it?" the foreman asked.

"Eva Martell and Adelle Winters are being prosecuted for the Hines murder on an information," said Mason. "I would suggest that while this Grand Jury is in session and has all of the witnesses present, it indict the *real* murderer."

"Who?" Gulling asked sarcastically.

"The assumption has always been that Robert Hines was murdered between five minutes of two and ten minutes past two, because at eleven minutes past two Adelle Winters left the apartment, carrying with her the gun with which Hines was killed."

"Well," the foreman asked, "what's wrong with that reasoning?"

"Everything," Mason said. "It isn't any of it true. The gun was found buried under garbage. Adelle Winters certainly didn't push it *down into* the garbage; yet no garbage was put in after the gun was deposited there. Just consider what that means."

"It doesn't mean a thing," Gulling said.

"Yes, it does," Mason said sharply. "It means that *somebody*—somebody not Adelle Winters—pushed that gun way down into the garbage *because* that somebody recognized the possibility that more garbage might have been deposited since the time when Adelle Winters had been seen looking inside. It means, therefore, that some person must have taken the gun out of the garbage can, used it, and *put it back*—and in putting it back pushed it well down into the garbage.

"Furthermore, it means that the person was somebody who knew that Adelle Winters had been seen at that spot. So far as I know, only two persons knew this. One of them is the detective, Tom Folsom; the other is the man who employed the Interstate Investigators to shadow Adelle Winters—Orville Reedley."

"Reedley has a perfect alibi for the time when the murder was committed—if that's what you're getting at," Gulling said.

"The time when you *think* the murder was committed," Mason corrected. "The time at which the murder was actually committed was some half-hour later than that. Orville Reedley, sitting in the office of the detective agency, got the report that Adelle Winters had left the apartment, had gone directly to the Lorenzo Hotel, had gone to a garbage can and raised the lid. He was curious to learn whether she had put anything into the garbage can. He left the agency's office, went at once to the hotel—using the alley entrance so as to be safe from observation—and found she had put a gun in the garbage.

"He wondered why Adelle Winters had left the apartment and taken pains to hide a gun so promptly. He took the gun and went up to investigate, knowing that both women were then out of the place. Evidently he had a pass-key he'd got hold of for just such a chance.

"Well, you can see how it looked to Reedley. There was Hines sitting in the bedroom in his shirt sleeves, making himself entirely at home. And remember—Reedley thought that the detectives were following his wife, and that the substituted brunette was the woman with whom he was madly in love. He had a gun in his pocket, and the thought must have suddenly flashed through his mind that, if he pulled the trigger on that gun and eliminated his rival, he had only to go back again to the hotel and push the gun down into the garbage can to make sure that somebody else would pay the penalty for *his* crime."

"Any proof of that wild theory?" Gulling asked.

"Fingerprints on the under side of the garbage-can cover," Mason said curtly. "You had your expert develop those prints, but your reasoning was so sloppy that you failed to check them with the witnesses' prints. You have your fingerprint expert here, and Orville Reedley is outside. I suggest that in just about five minutes you can determine whether you've got proof or not."

And, moving with calm assurance, Mason walked toward the door. Bowing to the foreman of the Grand Jury, he said, "I guess you gentlemen don't need me any more."

The foreman smiled. "Better wait until we get those fingerprints," he said.

21

Paul Drake and Della Street were sitting in Mason's private office when the lawyer unlocked the door and entered.

"Gosh, Perry," Paul Drake said, "it's ten o'clock. Did they give you a good sweating?"

Mason grinnned. "They sweated the truth out of me."

"What do you mean?"

Mason said, "I was darn near asleep at the switch, Paul. It took the jolt of your message about that key to jar me into realizing the truth."

"Go on. Shoot."

"We were all hynotized because we had been given an erroneous time factor. Because the murder was committed in the apartment house with a weapon that left that building at eleven minutes past two, we naturally assumed that the murder had been committed before that. And Adelle Winters didn't help any. She's a most terrible liar. Whenever the going gets rough she hides from the facts. Because she felt certain the murder had been committed while she was down in the lobby at the apartment house, she told about seeing an empty shell in the gun and smelling powder. Actually, she did no such thing, but she wanted to have some good reason which would explain why she ditched the gun and, of course, she felt certain the gun had been fired at that time."

"Hadn't it?"

"Gosh, no!"

"It was in the garbage pail after that."

"Actually the revolver made another trip back to the apartment house and then back to the garbage pail."

"Who did it?"

"Orville Reedley. He went to the hotel to see what Adelle Winters had been looking for in the garbage pail. Actually, he assumed she might have dropped something in and wanted to see what it was. He found a gun lying on top of the garbage. He was the only one who knew that the revolver was in the garbage pail. And as it happened, he was smart enough to realize that he could take that gun, go kill the man he wanted out of the way, and have a perfect setup to blame the crime on someone else. Where he slipped up was leaving the print of his right index finger and his ring finger on the inside of the metal handle on the garbage pail. Once they took his fingerprints and compared them with the developed latents on the garbage pail, there was nothing to it."

"How about the wallet that Adelle Winters took—if she did take it?" Della Street asked. "That's what's bothering me."

"It bothered me too," Mason admitted, "and it bothered Gulling. The story about that wallet is really good."

"What is is?"

"After Orville Reedley had pulled the trigger, he realized that he might plant a little additional evidence if he could make it appear that the body had been frisked. He knew that *someone* was going to discover the body; he thought it would be Adelle Winters. When he took the wallet from Hines's pocket there was only four hundred and fifty dollars in it, and he wasn't sure that would be considered enough to have tempted someone to steal the wallet. The person he was laying for all along, of course, was Adelle Winters. He felt certain she'd be back. Understand, he didn't know why the two women had left the apartment. It was his idea—as you know—that the woman who was occupying the place— the woman whose chaperone Adelle Winters was—was *his wife*. And it was Adelle Winters that he wanted to involve. So he cast some bread on the waters. He opened his own wallet, extracted thirty-one hundred dollars, pushed the bills into the wallet, then tossed the wallet into the bedroom

216

and closed the door. And Adelle Winters did exactly what he hoped she'd do.''

"Then Reedley must have confessed," Drake said.

"That's right," Mason told him. "When he was confronted with the fingerprint evidence, and as soon as it became evident that they really had a perfect case against him, he switched completely around with that emotional instability of his and told the whole story. The interesting part of it was that Gulling had another trump up his sleeve for me, just as I was afraid he might have. He tried to show that, because Adelle Winters was my client and because she had taken the wallet, under the law in regard to lost property that has been found, she was guilty of larceny. And that gave *me* a chance to play *my* trump card!"

"About Gulling's finding *your* wallet with the money and the 'code' letter in it?"

"Not exactly," Mason said. "I pulled that on him, but of course it was obviously a trap. I had meant it to be a dramatic courtroom gesture, in case he started an argument about the other wallet. The law provides that found property must be turned in within a 'reasonable' time, and I wanted to show what Gulling's idea of a 'reasonable' time was. Also, I knew he would waste a lot of energy trying to decipher the 'code' in the letter I had Della write by hand— really the *only* kind of code that can never in the world be deciphered."

"What kind is that?" Drake asked.

"A coded message that has no meaning," Mason replied with a grin. "But after they had Reedley's confession, I was in a beautiful position to teach Gulling some law."

"How do you mean?"

"Reedley admitted that he had put his own money in the wallet and tossed it on the floor. And because the money already there was in tens and twenties only, and Reedley wanted to have it all in bills of high denomination, he put that money in his pocket and replaced it with bills of his own before he tossed it on the floor. Therefore, when Adelle

Winters picked it up, she wasn't 'finding' anything within the meaning of the law."

"What was she doing?" Della Street asked.

"Taking possession of property that had been *abandoned*," Mason said. "There's quite a distinction in law between lost property and abandoned property. When Reedley tossed his own money on the floor, he had abandoned it.

"When property has been lost, the owner retains the title but is deemed to have parted with the property accidentally. When property has been abandoned, it is deemed to have returned to the public domain, and the first person who takes it into possession is entitled to retain not only the property itself but the title to it.

"Gulling is shrewd and keen, but he isn't a fast thinker. He got his feet wet trying to nail me as an accomplice on the purse business before I sprang my point. After I had sprung it, he recognized its logic, and that put him in a rather sorry light."

"And what was finally done with the money?" Drake asked.

"I told Adelle Winters I'd take fifteen hundred dollars as a fee, and she could keep the other sixteen hundred as a souvenir," Mason said. "And when I left, the Grand Jury were having a lot of fun. They all crowded around me, patted me on the back, and shook hands, and Gulling's blood pressure ran up to two hundred and fifty!

"But this case has been too darn close for comfort. Gosh, Paul, here we are with the solution of the whole case fairly dangling in front of our eyes, and we couldn't see it simply because we let that damn prejudiced assistant district attorney pick the time when *he* thought the murder must have been committed, and let him sell us on the idea. If I hadn't suddenly started questioning the basic fact of the time element, we'd have been in a sweet mess.

"At that, next time I run across anyone who is borrowing a brunette, I'm going to let him *keep* her!"

218